VINYL MOON

ALSO BY MAHOGANY L. BROWNE

Chlorine Sky

VINYL MOON

MAHOGANY L. BROWNE

CROWN

NEW YORK

Text copyright © 2022 by Mahogany L. Browne

Jacket art copyright © 2022 by Dubelyoo

All rights reserved. Published in the United States by Crown Books for Young Readers, an imprint of Random House Children's Books, a division of Penguin Random House LLC, New York.

Crown and the colophon are registered trademarks of Penguin Random House LLC.

Visit us on the Web! GetUnderlined.com

Educators and librarians, for a variety of teaching tools, visit us at RHTeachersLibrarians.com

Library of Congress Cataloging-in-Publication Data

Names: Browne, Mahogany L., author.

Title: Vinyl moon / Mahogany L. Browne.

Description: First edition. | New York: Crown Books for Young Readers, [2022] | Audience: Ages 14+ | Audience: Grades 10–12 | Summary: "A teen girl reeling from the scars of a past relationship finds healing and hope in the words of strong Black writers and the new community she builds in Brooklyn, New York"—Provided by publisher.

Identifiers: LCCN 2021032805 (print) | LCCN 2021032806 (ebook) | ISBN 978-0-593-17643-6 (hardcover) | ISBN 978-0-593-17644-3 (lib. bdg.) | ISBN 978-0-593-17645-0 (ebook)

Subjects: CYAC: Self-actualization (Psychology)—Fiction. | Books and reading—Fiction. | African Americans—Fiction. | Family violence—Fiction. | Schools—Fiction. | Brooklyn (New York, N.Y.)—Fiction.

Classification: LCC PZ7.1.B7977 Vi 2022 (print) | LCC PZ7.1.B7977 (ebook) | DDC [Fic]—dc23

The text of this book is set in 11-point Adobe Garamond.

Interior design by Ken Crossland

Printed in the United States of America

10 9 8 7 6 5 4 3 2 1

First Edition

This story is dedicated to the act of showing up for yourself. Every book I write is a love letter to the teachers who never gave up on me. This story is only possible because of my grandmother, the mighty Elsie Jean, and the gumption I inherited as a result of her backbone.

VINYL
MOON

Hello, Brooklyn . . . Goodbye, California

First day of school. East Coast. Brooklyn. And it's like I've never been alive like this before. I walk into Benjamin Banneker and the security guard asks me for my student ID. "It's—it's my first day," I stutter. Not because I'm afraid. But because I'm confused. I've never had to have ID to come onto a school campus before. This is real different than California. But after that weird night with my ex-boyfriend, Darius, my mom (she who I now call Elena) drove away with me in the front seat, tears falling down her cheeks as she whimpered, "You're moving to Brooklyn with your uncle Spence."

I was too numb to answer, my throat was a sea of sandpaper, and I couldn't even cry. All I can think of is: My eyes almost swollen. The fight. His Chevy Impala in the school parking lot. My arm. His furious eyes. His permanent scowl. The fight. My eyes closed against the light. All over some dumb argument during a school basketball game. So, when I mix my words, I think it makes me look guilty. I mean, it's my fault Darius got in trouble, right?

"Go to the left," the security guard directs me. He has a tapered fade and black-rimmed glasses. He is almost frowning at me. Maybe he thinks it's my fault too?

I walk into the office with the glass door covered by brightly colored flyers about the next PTA meeting, the importance of recycling, and something about an open mic night. I am a little surprised there is no bell to signal my arrival, but when the door recoils with a loud prison-door thud, I realize that is the signal itself. I sit in the first empty chair I see. The room is quartered off by a long plank of buffed wood, and there are metal baskets lined up against the wall with last names in front of them. Bernette, Chambers, Elliot, Frederick . . . I am reading the names silently when a brown-skinned woman with a yellow-printed headwrap and glasses latched to a golden chain around her neck walks into the office, where more mailboxes line the wall next to a vase of sunflowers that look back at me. *Golden globes of light,* Mom—I mean, Elena used to call them. They were her favorite.

My back and arm begin to ache. I blame these stupid chairs. You know the ones with wooden seats and cushioned backs? Like, who does that? Who wants to sit on something that looks like *I promise to hurt your ass, but your back is going to be nice and comfy!* I feel like it's a form of punishment, these chairs from medieval times. The woman with the African-print kaftan and headwrap looks me up and down and smiles.

"You must be Angel. It's so good to meet you! I'm Mrs. Barton. I'm the assistant to Principal Stern. You want some tea?" Mrs. Barton opens the cupboard, and it closes so quick I almost confuse it with the loud spring of the front office door.

"Hi, Mrs. Barton." I stand up slowly, reaching out to shake her hand with my left hand, the one hand that is still swollen but is not in the shoulder sling. She grabs my hand with both of hers lightly and squeezes. "No, I'm not thirsty," I say. "Thank you."

"You can call me Mrs. B. I'm so glad you made it! We've been waiting for you," she says, and it almost sounds like a song. "Let me know if you need anything, okay? I've got your class schedule here. Your temporary student ID." She walks back to a stack of papers and grabs a pale-yellow folder. "I thought we could wait a bit for the pictures. Is next week okay?" She eyes the bruise gleaming like a lightning strike near my right eye.

I nod slowly. *She must think it's my fault too.* That's the way guilt spreads. It makes me think about the little things again and again. It makes me slip around in my brain for hours, wondering if I did things this way or that way, maybe, just maybe, I wouldn't have messed my life up.

Rewind

I didn't have the best life in California, sure. But it was mine. I had my little brother, Amir, and the triplets: Ayanna, Ashanti, and Asha. I didn't have a lot of friends. Elena and I weren't on the best terms. But I was used to the life. Forever sun beaming in a sleepy town tucked in Northern California. People talked a lot of mess about me, but that's only because they didn't know me. They had to make up things or just jump to conclusions. It didn't bother me much. Because I had Darius. He made it all worth it. The way he looked at me for the first time.

I was waiting at a bus stop on my way to the mall. I wanted to take pictures with my "sometime" friends at the One Hour Photo. *You don't have to be good friends to take pictures,* Elena said. *Besides, you need to make memories while you can. You don't get a do-over button.* She was usually smoking a cigarette or smelling like a bunch of Clorox and arriving home tired. Her feet propped up on the seat of the kitchen chair. Her hands raw and tight after her day's shift.

Darius was driving in a tricked-out hooptie. Super clean, dipped in sparkly cobalt-blue paint. He didn't smile when he saw me. His light brown eyes just lit up and something in my stomach did a flip. And that was that. I honestly didn't think I would see him again. Little did I know he was following the bus until I got off at the mall entrance a few miles down. Darius: tall, bronze complexion, and lean like a basketball player. He sat on top of that sparkly car in the parking lot, like a cologne ad or something. And it looked like he was waiting for me. But I didn't want to assume I was the only person going to a mall on a Saturday, so I started to walk by him. Before I could poorly pretend I was too busy with putting my lip gloss back in my purse than checking for him, he called out, "I know this is weird. But I was waiting for you. Can I walk you to wherever you're going?"

Mrs. B taps her fingers against the plexiglass window before turning the silver knob and pulling open the steel-like door. Even the doors here look heavier. I move soundless behind Mrs. B, grateful for a minute to be walking in the shadow of someone that seems so brave. The woman behind the book-filled desk rises quickly.

"Hey, Mrs. B!" She smiles. They hug as if they are old friends, and I feel like I'm crashing a party or something. The two of them chat in floral patterns, speaking warmly with the same words and tones that pepper the air of Flatbush, Brooklyn. I look around the room and notice a circle of nine chairs in the middle of the classroom. Two columns of desks line the window, and backpacks or small purses occupy some of the chairs.

"Angel?" Mrs. B's voice nudges me from my surveillance.

"Yes?" I move closer to the two women.

"This is Ms. Greenaway," Mrs. B says, introducing us. "She is your homeroom/Advisory teacher and our favorite poetry teacher on campus." She beams.

Ms. Greenaway snorts. "I'm the ONLY poetry teacher on campus. Call me Ms. G." She squeezes Mrs. B's shoulders and continues at rapid speed, "I'm so happy to have you. Advisory serves as homeroom and is the first class of the day. All the girls have gone to hang up flyers around campus. They will be back any minute. We're having our first open mic and the group is excited! Do you perform at all, Angel?"

Her brown eyes pour into mine and suddenly I feel shy. Not shy like a baby, but shy like I'm not sure I want them to know I don't know who I am anymore, so I shake my head no.

Once, I found a book of Maya Angelou in the dollar bin at the secondhand bookstore and carried it on me for days. I didn't have a lot of time to read it. But it fit in my pocket and whenever I found myself alone with nothing to do, no trio to pick up, no Amir to clean up after, I'd read a page or two. Took me almost a whole semester but I did it. Darius snatched it from me when he felt I was ignoring him. Ripped it to pieces because he said I thought it was more important than our relationship.

One day, I was quiet. Next day, I had nothing to lose. But here I am. After losing everything and relocating to a city three thousand miles away from home. As my shoulder begins to ache, like a well-timed reminder of past mistakes, I try to shrug. I wish I could do it all differently. I just don't know how. The shrug pinches a nerve and I grimace, which probably looks like I'm not interested in anything Ms. G is talking about. But she nods. Unbothered, like she understands.

"No problem. We'll figure out something for you to do for participation credit. I have all kinds of amazing humans in here. Some of them sing, dance, rap, and spit poetry. And some of them draw or do hair or are really stylish and share tips!" She pulls at her long, bright earrings. They're a pair of colorful leather strings, each attached to a single silver button. "And if none of that sounds fun—I always need a stage manager! You're on time, right?" I nod. "Good," she laughs. "'Cause I need all the time-conscious people in my world that I can get!"

Mrs. B and Ms. G clap five with their hands and I walk away to the window where an empty desk sits. I drop my denim backpack and look out the barred window. Two floors up and all I can see is red and orange leaves. A breeze swings by and shakes the tree branches. I shudder.

Right now, in Cali, the weather is easily eighty degrees or hotter. I would be walking on campus with my new jean shorts, and maybe

Darius would have dropped me off. I would be entering my junior year of high school with my scalp covered in cornrow braids, because my cousin Alice is one of the best hair braiders around. I don't get to see her often because she lives over an hour away. But every summer we have a family reunion. We all pack up and go to a camping site near the Redwoods or Yellowstone, and we spend the weekend together. I hate camping. But I love my cousins. It's the only time we get to see each other, because it seems our parents, who are first cousins, got a weird-ass rivalry that keeps them far, *far* away from each other. Elena says it's because Mae thinks she's better than everyone and always has an opinion about how she raises us kids. The triplets have a different father than me and Amir, so when we have the chance to all be together, it's important. When they're with their dad, me and Amir fend for ourselves. My mom, Elena, spent most of her life trying to prove to everyone that she belonged, and she made some real bad decisions. Now she works pickup jobs wherever she can to make ends meet, and during school hours she works as a custodian.

People used to make jokes about her job, but I couldn't care less. Before Amir got into the magnet school, the jokes about Elena bothered him. "She's still our mom," he would grumble. Amir is a sensitive genius. "STEM Kid from the Stars" is what I call him. The only thing we share is our hair color and light eye color. We got that from our dad. I'm not as smart as Amir, and he's only two years younger than me. I think I'm more like Elena than our dad in that way. Damn, I haven't thought of my dad in so long. It feels like a test I didn't prepare for, and it brings up too many bad memories. I shake my head, like the branch caught in the middle of the wind, as Mrs. B calls me back.

"Angel, here is your schedule. Someone from Advisory will take you through the rest of your day. Ms. G, I've got to get back. But call me if you need!" And she's out the door, a fragrance of mango shea butter and sunflowers in her wake.

Ms. G smiles. "In the beginning of class, we do a check-in. This way the class can know how you're feeling. It's easy, use the scale one-to-ten. Just so folks know how you are, ya know? Some days I'm a five! I'm just happy I made it to class on time. And some days, I had a good cup of chai and I'm fearless, honey! I'm a nine! But there is no wrong answer, okay?"

I nod. My left hand still holding close, my right arm in the sling.

Ms. G looks at my arm. "And you don't have to talk about anything you don't want to. Take your time. This is the classroom where we get to just be. The world is hard enough, Angel. This is your safe space. And the students in this room, they become like family and they are all excited to meet you." She finishes just as the classroom door opens and the students of H.E.R. Leadership Advisory file into the room.

Have You Ever?

Held your breath?
Because you were afraid
of what might come out
when you exhale

That's how it feels to be me

Holding my breath
and swinging for the fences

Swinging for my own life

Once upon a time
I was just a girl with a crew of younger look-alikes

Once upon a time
I was just a girl growing into a teenager
My mom worked her fingers to the bone

But she didn't know she also worked my name to dust

Once upon a time
I stopped holding my breath

I took a deep deep breath

I inhaled all of the doubt

And started to believe everyone before I believed in myself

"Yerrrrrrrr," a voice wails as the room begins to fill up with a half dozen or so different faces. One girl is wearing two Afro puffs and a kimono outfit with shiny black punk rock–style platform shoes. Her makeup is impeccable, and her eyes got this real perfect black line swooshed at the top of each eyelid. "Hey," she says to me before taking her seat near a Starbucks cup with a chai string hanging from the top.

"Hey," I squeak. *Damn, did I squeak?*

I'm so done with myself that I start rummaging through my backpack. It's a bad habit; I make myself busy when I'm nervous. I think it's because I have too many emotions to manage. I grab my yellow zip-up sweatshirt and find an empty seat in the circle.

"Take off the hat in class, July," Ms. G orders.

A girl in a fitted Yankees cap walks to Ms. G's desk and places her crown on top of a small stack of papers. "We gonna need more, Ms. G," she bellows. Her tan Carhartt vest and black jeans with black construction boots catch my eye. And her style is straight fire. She pours confidence. "Hey, Angel!" She yells my name like she knew I was coming. Like we're already friends.

"Hey," I say, no less squeaky but more certain. I've really got to get it together. This room is full of cool kids. I don't think I was prepared.

Another girl in tight red leggings with a matching crop top peeking from beneath a flannel shirt sits next to Ms. G's desk. Her hand rests on the shoulder of the girl in the Carhartt vest. She wiggles her index finger at me, and I already know what this is. I nod and wave a little with my free hand.

"Okay, everybody. Get in the circle. We want to welcome Angel to the group correctly," Ms. G instructs. She sits in the seat with a special cushion tossed on the base of the plastic frame.

"Angel, this is H.E.R. Leadership Advisory. Kamilah, can you tell Angel what H.E.R. stands for, please?" Ms. G opens a notebook with lined paper and flicks her pen alive.

"H.E.R. stands for Her Excellence is Resilience and Honoring Everyone's Roots," a girl with deep bangs and wearing all black responds with little to no emotion. She isn't mean. She just doesn't seem to want to be bothered.

"Or," Carhartt Vest adds, "Hip-hop in its Essence and Real." She chuckles and sits down next to Ms. G, her Yankees-fitted positioned on her knee.

"Thank you, Kamilah, and thank you for that historical nod at hip-hop, Ju Ju. I appreciate you." Ms. G smiles. "Angel, we are all here for the first forty-five minutes of the day. Everyone, please introduce yourself and tell the group how you feel today using the scale of one-to-ten. We'll start with you, Ju Ju."

"My name is July. Because it's the hottest month of the year. Just like me. But you can call me Ju Ju. Like that ain't got no flavor!" She smiles at the Girl in Red and continues, "I'm feeling good, Ms. G. I'm like an eight or a nine. I got my classes changed so I can get up out this school before two p.m.! Senioritis is kicking in and I don't want to play myself. Also, Nikki here and me are working on our senior hustle together. I'm working on this app for sneaker heads. So hopefully, this time next year, when I've graduated, I'm working at Google or living in Silicon Valley or something. Nahmeen?"

Everyone laughs except me. I hate Silicon Valley. It's super-rich people, and they took over the area so fast that the landlords and the taxes started moving out working-class families. These are the same families who are making a living carrying two and three jobs and have to move to more affordable living areas. But you need a car. Think of that! No car plus living in the boonies equals hard living. Silicon Valley makes it so expensive to live, now people living out in far-out suburbs named Mountain View and Antioch. (Which is another word for gentrification. *Nahmeen?*)

"My name is Eva." A brown-skinned girl with big cheeks and sad eyes smiles. She's wearing a red-blue-and-yellow Polo-style windbreaker and a pair of clean white Air Force 1s. "I'm from Queens so my commute here is stupid." Everyone laughs except me. "I'm feeling like a seven today, Ms. G." She looks out the window. "Life is real boring and folks get caught up on that social media life, I'm off it."

"Don't listen to her!" Ju Ju interrupts. "She's Instagram famous! She got mad followers. It's crazy. I'm waiting for her to put me on, so my sneaker app can really blow."

Eva rolls her eyes and continues, "That's the thing. I like talking about real things. And I like being real with people. But the IG fame or whatever only brings out trolls. I'm still trying to figure out how to dial back a little bit. I like talking about things online with folks from Tokyo to PS 13, but the trolls, yo! You can only block so many of 'em." She crosses her legs and shrugs.

"They call me T. Short for Teiya," the girl in the kimono says next, cupping her tea and looking directly at me. "I'm feeling okay. Maybe a six. Nothing bad or good has happened. I think that's okay." Ms. G nods and the rest of the circle nods with her.

"I'm RaChelle. It's like Michelle. But not," a girl with blue braids and pink-rimmed glasses says. She has on the longest sweater I've ever seen, black leggings, and a pair of stacked white leather Converse. I smile. Because it's the first time I've seen anything that I recognize from Cali. I have the same pair at home. "I feel like, I don't know." She stops. She removes the glasses from her face and rubs her eyes.

Her nails are painted teal with diamond sparkles accenting her two pinkies. I think, *Anyone with those nails owns the world!* RaChelle sighs. "I guess I'm a seven or eight. Me and bae got into it last night and I'm just over it."

My stomach does a flip and instantly I think about Darius.

"Who's next?" Ju Ju interrupts again, and RaChelle puts her glasses back on and pouts at Ms. G.

"That's enough, Ju Ju. No more interruptions, ay?" Ms. G puts her pen down. Her eyes are a soft and welcoming brown, but the way she squints—it looks like she isn't here for games.

"It's all good, Ms. G." RaChelle rolls her eyes. "It's always the Ju Ju Show up in this bitch." She flings her hands in the air.

"Excuse me." Girl in Red straightens. And I realize it's the first time I've heard her voice.

"Anyways," another girl begins. She has long curly bangs with a part in the middle and two long rope braids on each side. "My name is Reina. I'm from Bushwick. My mother is from Bushwick. I'm Brooklyn through and through." She wipes her hands like that's that. "I am feeling like a good nine today. Your turn, Nikki." Reina sits back. A hand on each knee and her eyes looking directly to her left.

"I'm feeling ight." Nikki is the Girl in Red. She gives a side-eye to RaChelle, who isn't paying a bit of attention to her. Then her eyes rest on Ju Ju and she smirks. "I'm like a nine today, because I got plans to go to the pier and just chill with my heart." She looks smugly at Kamilah to her right.

"Well, I'm next." Kamilah rustles with her backpack. "I'm great. If you don't need sleep and whatnot." She shrugs. Her flannel shirt falls open a little, revealing a small wet spot on the front of her black Rolling Stones T-shirt. "Avion hasn't been sleeping well. My son," she directs to me. "He's teething and cranky. But that's my heart. So, I'm the usual eight." Dropping her bag after retrieving a baby wipe, she begins to dab at her shirt. Gives up and tosses the wipe in the still-open bag.

I take a gulp. Everything feels like it's moving in slow motion. But I don't want to cause a scene. For the past five weeks, I've been working on breathing slow. The social worker said it helps with something called PTSD. "I'm Angel," I croak.

"We know that part!" Ju Ju excitedly offers. "Where you from? What's good with you?"

"Relax," Nikki says.

"Ju Ju, let her talk." Ms. G coaches, "Go ahead, Angel. We have spent the last couple of weeks together, so folks know each other a bit more. Tell us whatever you want us to know. If it's just about how you're feeling today, that's okay. If you want to talk about where you're from and what you're into—maybe a song that's in rotation—that's good too!"

Ms. G stretches, lifting her arms in the air and wiggling her fingers toward the ceiling. Like no pressure. But she can't feel the elephant-sized weight sitting on my chest.

I close my eyes and almost touch the bruise before I stop. I remember the worst parts of my memories when I least expect it. I open my eyes, and everyone is staring.

I start, "I've been living here for five weeks now. It's so different from California, where I'm from. Um, today I feel like a four. I'm just trying to get my footing. I miss my little brother and sisters too much. Um, I've been listening to Summer Walker on repeat." I smile.

"Word! Summer Walker's song 'Riot' is crazy!" Ju Ju offers.

"That is my jam," RaChelle agrees.

And the murmur ripples around the circle like an eel, slick and quick. I feel the weight loosening, like an anchor falling into the dark water; the chain, thick and heavy, slips easy until something beneath gives way.

2nd Period: Botany Science

I try not to smile when I walk out of Ms. G's room. She gives me my manila folder and instructs Eva to walk me to my next class.

Eva is nice enough. She's quiet, and her head is down in her cell phone as she scrolls her Twitter feed. I'm a bit in awe. She seems to really have it all together. "People are so ridiculous." She locks her iPhone screen and stuffs it into her jeans pocket.

I nod. Because it's not like she asked my opinion. But I agree. People can be overwhelming.

"So, you moved from Cali, huh?" Her attention is on me as we walk down the hall. It's like organized chaos. Two rows go in opposite directions; a well-planned traffic jam. I match her stroll. I don't really know where I'm going so I enjoy the walk until . . .

"Watch it!" she yells to a guy who bumps into my good arm. He's obviously going against the grain and doing whatever he wants. His earbuds are stuck in one ear and a skateboard is peeking from his backpack.

"Damn, sorry, Eva!" he says over his back. Before looking at me, who he actually should be apologizing to, and stumbling into a locker. I snatch my attention away and focus on Eva, who chuckles.

"Girl, that's just Sterling. He ain't got no equilibrium. I'm surprised he can skateboard."

We finally get to room 308 and I gasp. It's like walking into another world. There are plants everywhere, like a full-blown jungle. And against the wall, quartered off by gates, is a table full of lamps. Eva turns to me and smiles. "I'll return to walk you to your next class, okay?"

I feel like a burden. "You don't have to. I can find my way."

She shakes her head. "Nah, sis. I'm right next door. I gotchu. We have literature together. Don't worry about it." She turns on her heel and walks out.

I look around the room and I feel dizzy. Like I am in my body but not. It's so surreal here. I've never seen such a mixture of cultures, styles, and sounds. Back home we all kind of wore the same jeans, hoodie, and Converse combination. Some of us mixed it up if we came from money and wore a variety of Vans. But the outfit was pretty much the same. But here—everyone is so beautiful and different. The smells are like home, but not. It's crisp and green and smells like grass with newly turned soil. I walk by a row of plants and I want to touch them, but there is a sign that says, DON'T TOUCH! I snatch my good hand away, like I'm in a museum or something. I walk to the last row, where there is an empty seat, but before I can sit down, I hear my name.

"Hi, Angel, I'm Mr. Jackson." A man with a beard and bald head walks from the front of the classroom. "That seat is open, but you won't be able to hear me well when the music gets to playing for the plants." He nods to the DON'T TOUCH! sign.

I saw the sign, but not the two sets of boom boxes nearby with foam headphones plugged into each base. I move to a seat he suggests and am immediately nervous again. It's not the front, but it's the center. I'm afraid I'll feel like the room is closing in on me. You know that weird feeling of the walls coming closer and the voices getting louder? But then I look at the plants and take a deep breath. Mr. Jackson starts introducing the lesson and walks over to me with a textbook and a black wired notebook. He places them both on my desk and taps the top gently.

"Page thirty-five, everyone. Let's finish our annotated reading about the difference between controlled environments and traditional farming." I take another deep breath and turn the pages until I find my place.

3rd Period: Literature

As promised, Eva is waiting outside Mr. Jackson's door.

She looks up from her phone. "Hey, you ready?" she asks.

"Yeah." I nod. "Lit is next, right?" We fall into the line of bodies moving toward a door with a red EXIT sign painted above the doorframe.

"Yes, ma'am. This class is dope. It's all about revolutionary literature. It's an advanced course, so we get to read Toni Morrison, James Baldwin, June Jordan, Lorraine Hansberry, and Walter Dean Myers." I nod again, like I've heard these names before. I have no idea who she's talking about.

It isn't that I don't like reading. (It's just that I've never had much room to do anything for myself.) Amir got to do it all. Read, write, play ball. Hell! He got a scholarship for that smart kids' school, and it's like everything around us revolved around him and The Trio. I was never mad about it. Elena let me try out modeling once or twice, and when it didn't catch on, I just figured my turn to try new things was over. Elena (she hates when I call her by her first name) says I think I'm grown. But ever since we fell out over Darius, I felt like I lost my mom. So now she's just Elena.

Amir though? He's a star. Curly-headed with hazel eyes. People are always so drawn to him. When he was little, I would carry him around like a doll. I would do anything for him.

I'm not mad about how differently things turned out for us. He's probably at that fancy school wearing a suit and tie. (It's the school's policy to dress like you work in a Fortune 500 company.)

While I'm stuck here. Living in Brooklyn and missing the afterschool hangouts at the Chinese food spot a block away from school, or the long sessions of cigarettes and soda pop in the parking lot of the skating rink. I miss the football games and all that green grass. We climb our way up two flights of stairs and I'm winded. I take a deep breath and start coughing. It smells like fresh paint and boys' locker room. Yuck.

I didn't realize how buildings took up space in New York City. My old high school had a campus with buildings spread everywhere. There was only one building that was three floors high. Nothing like this. Everything is in one building and six stories high with each window barred, like prison. There is so much sky and sun I don't get to see.

My uncle Spence says, *You never get used to it.* He left over twenty years ago, before Elena lost herself in boyfriends and other bad decisions.

Uncle dislikes my father, Ray, a lot. Even though I've been told I look just like him. When I look in the mirror, I see that man's face: thick eyebrows and sharp greenish-gray eyes. When I look in the mirror, I see the face of a man that no one loves, and I think this is exactly why Elena sent me here.

She said I needed to be around men who know how to treat women. I don't even know what that means. But I'm so tired of arguing. Besides, life began to happen so fast around me that I felt like, *What the hell. I'll go live in Brooklyn for a while.* I'll figure out how to get back later. But for now, this is me.

I must look spaced out—the way I caught Eva staring at me with a weird look. Before she goes back to scrolling her phone, she taps the seat next to her. I plop down and check out the basketball court through the barred window.

Tired of reminiscing about parents that I didn't choose. Tired of the day, already.

Who Are You When No One Is Looking?

I think about Amir and he always knows who he is:

Brilliant

Mom's only son

My rock

I think about Darius and he always knows who he is:

Strong

Stubborn

Firstborn

My rock

Before everything changed

I didn't need to think about who I am

I am Angel

I am me

I like ocean bonfires and sweet tea with a little bit of lemonade

Before everything changed

I didn't really think about who got me

I had Amir

I had The Trio

I even had Elena

On my side

Before everything changed

It wasn't about sides

But about sound

I could hear the music in everything

Elena let me play with her record player

The one with the loose arm

Arm so loose you had to put a quarter on top of the metal bar

Arm so loose it would skip and swim across the vinyl without

George Washington's silhouette sitting blameless on top

4th Period: Gym

The bell rings and it's like I'm transported to a totally different world. Eva loves this class. She's like *smart* smart. Not just fashionable! She's quoting Baldwin (she calls him Jimmy) and someone named June Jordan and I'm constantly scribbling notes. I'm not sure if I love the class yet. After the echo begins to clear out the classroom, I scramble to gather my things, and Eva is still talking to the teacher, Ms. Seary. They are nodding excitedly and before I know it, we're out the door.

Everyone at this school is so sure of themselves, which makes me double nervous about who I am.

Angel: ash-brown hair smoothed into a messy bun, check. Medical blue sling, check. Black high-top Converse, black ripped jeans, and a bright yellow hoodie that reads *Cali;* check, check, check.

Uncle Spence said we could go school shopping when he gets paid this weekend, so I'm stuck with old outfits from back home. Here, I'm like a sore thumb. Sure, I was able to secure some Eco Style hair gel and a little toothbrush. This made my baby hair game look decent. But I still don't know if I belong. Uncle Spence said it'll be that way for a while.

It's like he knows what I'm thinking before I ever say a word. He says it's 'cause I'm his firstborn niece and he spoiled me. He looks like Elena, except his freckles are more spectacular. He has a bald head with one of the most perfect sets of teeth you've ever seen. He says I have his smile, and I laugh. I only have a sweep of freckles across my nose, but I powder it ghost so no one can really see them unless I'm barefaced. And with these bruises still shining, I doubt I will be foundation free for a bit longer.

Eva smiles. "You think a lot, huh, Angel?"

And I avert my eyes, embarrassed to be caught running around in my own head again. "Yeah. I think I had so many changes so quickly that I'm just trying to tack some things down."

"Word," she says, frowning at my arm. "You almost ready to eat?"

"Wait, what?" I stop walking. "It's just ten-forty-five in the morning!"

"They stagger lunch period here because three different schools have to share the same cafeteria. Cafeteria opens at ten-forty-five, eleven-thirty, and twelve-fifteen. Your lunch time is right smack-dab in the middle. And they don't play that leave campus and come back mess for anyone but maybe the seniors. So, get used to it. But after gym, that's where you will go. I've got work-study with Mrs. B. But there are signs to the gym. You need me to walk you or you good?"

"That's crazy!" I respond, and squint furiously at the class schedule on the crumpled paper, still thinking about this eating schedule from hell.

"Don't trip." She laughs. "You got this. The stairs are right behind you. Gym is in the basement. They don't expect you to participate, so I would suggest you request a transfer to Mrs. B. She has odd jobs here and there." She shrugs. Her windbreaker makes noise when her shoulders drop.

"Thanks so much, Eva." She waves and is walking around the corner back toward the entrance of the school.

I turn on my heel and hurry down the stairs to follow the signs that point toward the girls' locker room. *It's too early for a gym class.* And already I'm thinking of what the gym teacher might say when they see my arm. I don't have the energy to talk about what I can and can't do. I got this bad boy on for two more weeks; then I'm free. I almost smile. I knock on the plexiglass window of an office situated between a set of locker rooms. A woman wearing a white polo shirt, white basketball shorts, and white sneakers calls me into the taupe-colored cubed room. A quick meeting in Coach Bernette's office and I'm already redirected to attend the meditation class.

Coach Bernette says, "It'll probably be best suited for your current condition." She motions to my arm. Then, for the first time in a long time, an adult asks me what I want to do.

"Do you want to check with Mrs. Barton and see if Ms. Lena has space?"

No one asked me if I wanted to move here. No one asked me if I loved Darius. No one asked me what happened. Everyone just made a decision to move me out in the middle of the night after I was released from the emergency room. A social worker was there when we left, and a set of police officers.

Coach Bernette is still chewing and looking at me quizzically.

"I, uh, I've never meditated before," I begin. "But I'll try it. Sure."

Speak Up

Is what I would like to do

But it's hard to speak when glue closes your mouth tight

In the hospital

I see the world happening around me

A sling on my arm

My back against the cold white sheets

Everyone's eyes on me

Darius is nowhere to be found

Elena is crying and shaking her head

I am stone

I stopped crying so long ago

But I still feel everything

I feel the breeze when someone walks by and swishes my curtain
closed for privacy

I feel the tightness around my shoulder as it stretches up vine-like to
my neck

I feel my hair, the brown baby hairs now small Afro puffs forming

I feel the world moving and I can't keep up

I close my eyes

My mouth is dry

My mouth is dry and closed like a lock

Especially when the cops come to the side of my bed

As much as I want to speak up for myself

I know too much has happened

I know there is no going back

What is lost if you never knew what was missing?

What is a question that has no answer?

It's me.

It's me.

After School: DeKalb Avenue & Adelphi

The rest of the day moves slow as a sloth. I am able to switch my gym period to work-study with Mrs. B. Eva is gone and running errands as I stuff envelopes for some PTA meeting for the entire period. I float through the next couple of periods after lunch, including algebra, social science, and drama. My first day and I feel worn down. My arm aches, but at least the sun is out when school is over. When I finally exit the door, I almost want to scream. I just can't deal with many more "new student, whodis" vibes.

Instead, I pull my hood over my head and walk quickly toward the park. I need to be around some green trees and grass. Besides, this is the only place I know how to get to by heart. Fort Greene Park. I remember sneaking out to watch Spike Lee films and couldn't wait to see it for myself. I would watch the movies because I thought I might see my uncle Spence on the screen, walking home in his scrubs or drinking coffee in the background.

It's nothing like I thought it would be. The green park is filled with a bunch of white people and their perfectly manicured lapdogs. There is a set of tennis courts and a hill that is calling my name. I climb up the hill and trip over a rock. I regain my footing but not before I trip again and decide it's the universe telling me to sit the hell down.

I pull off my backpack and thud. I remove the sling from around my neck and the sensation of my skin waking back up begins to tingle. I just need to stretch it a little. I rotate my right hand. Counterclockwise like the doctor instructed. I try to wiggle my fingers and extend my arm, holding my elbow with my left palm. I shield my eyes a bit and watch the day-care school waddle their line of toddlers through the grass toward the seesaw, spin top, and swing set enclosed inside a plastic gate. Half a dozen tiny-sized humans hold their own red handle attached to a yellow rope, and they are so giddy I smile. I remember being that kind of happy. Before people could get into your head and make you doubt yourself. I close my eyes and face the sun.

"What are you doing?" a deep voice questions. My face flushed from all the heat, I shield my eyes and look toward the direction of the voice. When my eyes finally focus, they settle on Sterling, Skater Guy from the hallway. He's wearing a gray sweatshirt with *Dreamville* written across his chest, a pair of Vans, and fitted jeans. He doesn't mind that I look him over. Because it's obvious he's been looking at me bathe in the light.

"Just getting some sun," I answer quickly. "Why? You want to run into me again?"

"Yo. I just came to say my bad." He carries the skateboard with one hand holding a set of red wheels. His other hand opens up, showing his empty palm. "I didn't realize . . ." His voice trails off and he points to the shoulder sling resting on my lap.

"It's all good." I sigh. I close my eyes and move my hand back to my lap. Before I can turn my face to the sun again, Sterling starts.

"So, what's your name?"

I lower my eyes to look at him again. *I'm not interested,* I tell myself. And I am about to tell him the same except he has soft eyes. Like he might tear up when commercials about going away to college and missing your pet come on the television. It's kind of nice to see a guy with eyes like Amir's and my uncle Spence's baby pictures. And looking at him even closer now, I can tell he didn't mean to hurt me. Before I can open my mouth . . .

"Mind your business, Sterling!" a voice from behind him yells. Reina's hands are on her hips as she cackles. "If you don't go on somewhere! Ain't nobody got time." She moves past him with a stroller and sits down near the edge of the hill. A couple of feet behind Sterling is Kamilah, carrying a small bundle on her right hip.

I scoot down the hill, closer to Reina. Careful not to hurt my arm, which is good because then I don't have to focus on Sterling, who is still looking at me with those soft eyes. Like he is waiting for an answer.

"Sterling, get your nephew," Kamilah calls. And within seconds, he drops the skateboard, leans it on the stroller, and picks up a small brown-skinned baby in a furry teddy bear suit.

"Hey, big man!" he exclaims, and holds the little face near his. Sterling lifts the baby in the air like a bench press and a smile spreads across his face, all the way up to those eyes. He walks away toward the enclosed gates with the swing set. His question never answered.

Kamilah sits down next to Reina. "What y'all over here talking about?" She releases her bun of single inch-wide box braids and they fall down her back like a black waterfall. Her shirt is crumpled, but her spirit is bright.

"Sterling was definitely trying to holler," Reina explains as she flips open her cassette-tape clutch purse and grabs a piece of gum. She offers us each one. I decline. *Gum is bad for your teeth,* Uncle Spence reminds me.

"That lunch of chicken tenders was horrible. Like, who do they think they are? Feeding us that mess? I'm going to start bringing in a sandwich from the bodega." She shakes her head. Reina looks over toward the playground full of babies and pops her gum before smiling bright. She has a diamond on her tooth. It sparkles in the light.

"Oh, Sterling." Reina sighs.

Kamilah says, "That's my little brother. He's sweet. But I don't know if he's ready for anything more than skateboards and the SATs, girl."

I grimace. "Don't worry. He was just apologizing for running into my arm this morning."

"Oh shit! Sterling!" Reina yells. "Watch where the hell you're going!" Kamilah joins her in unison.

"Sorry, girl," Kamilah responds. "He got tunnel vision for real."

I giggle. "Avion is so cute. How old is he?"

"Nine months old next week." She smiles. "That little boy breaks my heart every day, he's so damn cute! Except when he can't sleep." She stretches her legs and smooths out her black leggings.

"He's got the cutest dimples," Reina adds, twirling one of her rope braids with red bobos at each end.

"Man . . . I miss my sisters," I say, looking ahead at nothing in particular. "I remember when they were that age. I used to put them to sleep and just look at them. It was better than watching TV. They're five now and refuse to sit still." I go silent.

"What's their names?" Reina asks.

"Ayanna, Ashanti, and Asha." I start plucking the grass turning brown.

"You got other siblings?" Kamilah asks. Her eyes dart over to her son and brother.

"Yep. A brother. He's two years younger than me and a genius. He attends one of those fancy schools where they wear ties and sports jackets. I'm the only one here. Me and my uncle. He moved here twenty years ago, and basically he's the only family I got." I toss the dead grass from my hand and wipe it on my jeans. "I better go," I say, putting the sling back in place and standing up slowly. "I'll see y'all tomorrow."

"Okay, girl," Reina and Kamilah chime.

"You okay?" Kamilah asks as I slowly climb down to the concrete.

My eyes water and threaten to spill everywhere. I nod. Wave goodbye and head toward Brooklyn Hospital. I decide to walk by Junior's and get a cheesecake. Then I follow the streetlights all the way up Fulton Street toward Crown Heights until everything is a blur.

Junior's on DeKalb & Flatbush Extension

Have you ever had a cheesecake so amazing it makes your mouth water just thinking about it? Junior's cheesecake is that and more. The cherry cheesecake, red velvet cheesecake, and dulce de leche caramel cheesecake are my favorites. I leave the original cheesecake for the tourists.

The orange-and-white cake boxes line the back wall when you walk through the glass doors. And there are three lines with three attendants waiting to get you out of their way. Folks stand in a sort of spiral and look like they are praying for a chance to score the new Jordans. Luckily, the employees have a hurry-up-and-go mentality. I'm in and out in seven minutes flat. I have a twenty-dollar bill to last me the week and today is only Tuesday. This cheesecake is going to take half of that. But I don't care. What do they say on Instagram—#SelfCare?

Meditation Be Like

You got yourself

You got yourself

You got to grab ahold of yourself sometimes and just hold on

You got to stop hearing the bad

You got to stop storing the bad in the bag next to your heart

You got to let it go

You can only control your reaction

You can only control your field of vision

You got yourself

You ain't got to have nobody

But if you got you

You got the gold

You win

You a winner

You got yourself

You got it

You got the park walks, if you are lucky

You got sweet desserts, if you are looking

You got the sauce and the swag

You got it all even when it feels like you got nothing

You got it

It is you

You got it

It is you

You know your name

You know your dreams

You got the power to change whenever you choose

You got the power to choose

You

Remember

Do you remember?

What is your favorite song?

Sing that

What is your favorite color?

Wear that

Who is your friend?

Tell them you love them

Then look in the mirror

Now say it again

Even the weirdest things are still here

Because they have a name

Like you

Even the strangest things are still here

Because they have a name

Like you

Even the loneliest room is a room

Like you

Alone is not lonely

Because you have you

The world is not complete

All its vibrations and sensations

All its sounds and smells

All its lessons calling us to the front of the class

Hold on

I Buy My Very Own Big-ass Slice of Cherry Cheesecake

Pull the orange-and-white-splattered plastic bag aside and stab my plastic fork into the container. I shove one full bite of cherries and filling with a little bit of crust into my mouth, close my eyes, and hum. I probably look crazy. But I don't care how I look.

This. Is. The. Food. Of. Gods.

And just one bite takes away my desire to cry in public, so it's a win-win. I want to eat the rest of this cake, but I decide I won't be that greedy yet. I'll go home and watch some YouTube with my little bit of happy. The long walk home allows me to kill the minutes that grow legs until hours, as I wait for Uncle Spence to get off from his shift at Kingsbrook Hospital over in East Flatbush.

After Uncle Spence graduated from his nursing program in California, he decided to move as far away as possible. He's been an X-ray technician working and living in Brooklyn ever since. Uncle Spence is a stand-up dude. He comes home in his scrubs with creases on his face. But he still has time to crack jokes with me. And he's always in a good mood, even when it's a bad day. He says, *You have to love what you do and then it's not just work but your passion.*

He says he loves working around people that look like him, giving them the best care when so many places turn them away. He refuses to take the raises they've tried to give him to go work in Manhattan. He says it's important for him to work in his borough and I should find something that moves me too. When I first arrived, he asked me with that gruff voice of his, his California accent long gone, *Whatchu trying to do with your life, Ang?* I told him I don't know. And he didn't miss a beat. *Now's the time to figure it out, niece. And I'm going to help you.*

Uncle Spence	Elena
Is a lighthouse	Is a flashlight
Is a fixture	Moves how the wind goes
Is the man	Is the woman I don't want to grow up to become

Uncle Spence	Elena
Got a plan	Never has a plan
Ain't playing games	Hates games too
Ain't been home since everything changed	Ain't left home and it changed her for the worse

Uncle Spence / Mom Elena

Is a strong wind

Is a broken home

Is the only light I see

When I am lost in the dark

& just trying to find my way

The corner of President and Franklin is unlike anything I've ever seen before. There are four bodegas (where I'm from we call them "corner stores"—yes, even if they aren't on the corner but located in the middle of the block), with all kinds of fruits stacked on the outside for easy picking. There is a coffee shop chain with orange and hot-pink lettering and a takeaway fried chicken joint called Roy's Hot & Crispy. Directly across from Roy's is Golden Crust Jamaican Bakery with bronzed, sun-streaked stacks of meat- and cheese-filled empanadas glowing in the window. And next to that are two different liquor stores, both with bulletproof glass encasing the shop, and one small church with its metal gates shuttered. There is a pizza shop called Butch's Surprise that still has the grand-opening banner over its door, but it's so fancy when Uncle Spence and I walked by, he scoffed and said, *I'm good on them fancy ten-dollar slices. I'll go to Not Ray's, where I know they made the sauce with love. Get a whole damn pie for that price.*

I love this block. All the hipsters crawl from the subway into an undisclosed bar. People just off work carry their items in sacks toward various shops. They talk like neighbors. Like people who like each other enough to remember one another's names. Some teens sit on benches near the major intersection and crack jokes on each other.

I wear my earbuds for moments like this. Uncle Spence got me a new iPhone and the family plan. Only thing I have to do is answer his texts and make no purchases in the App Store without notifying him. I don't mind. I stream SoundCloud and let the music transport me back home.

I follow this one DJ, DJ JiggyStax. He mixes old funk tracks, new R&B soul, and some hidden Afrobeat gems. I don't know the names of all the songs he plays, but the underground rappers make it sound like something familiar and something different. It reminds me of dancing with Elena and my dad when I was so young.

People say they lose themselves in music. I listen to JiggyStax's screwed EDM mix with Kendrick Lamar and stuff my hands into my pockets. I start my walk up the block toward the apartment. Let the rhythm and his words carry me home. *They got me frustrated, indecisive and power trippin' / Sour emotions got me lookin' at the universe different.*

Sure, some people may lose themselves in the melody. But not me. I find myself in music.

Music Makes

Everything

Everything

Everything

Feel like a motion picture: grainy film magic

full of memories I can't remember on my own

When I listen to music

I'm teleported back to when I was three

and I can see my mother and father

Back when they loved each other

Back when they would dance together

In the living room as I pretended to be asleep

On the brown corduroy couch

The record player never skipped

Stylistics on the vinyl merry-go-round

Sweet sweet in the air as they swayed

You make me feel brand-new

When I listen to music

I remember the way they held each other

Like a promise

Like a wish come true

And I peeked out to watch them

Like a spy

Like if they knew I was awake

they would stop holding on

A One-and-a-Half Bedroom in Brooklyn

I don't have a real room. It's like a closet. It fits my twin bed from Ikea. The same one I went to pick with Uncle Spence in an hour-rental U-Haul truck. I got a side table with a lamp and a set of three drawers. And I got pillows. Lots of pillows. The room can't hold much else. So, when I saw a beanbag in the children's section, I begged Uncle Spence. He laughed and threw it in the cart on top of my other pillows and new comforter set. I have a library card and one book.

A slightly used copy of poems by Maya Angelou.

Uncle Spence said it got him through some lonely spells when he was missing home the most. I haven't cracked it open yet. I guess I'm not feeling so lonely, yet.

I toss my bag on the floor, pull my sneakers off using the heel-to-toe method, and lift my arm out of the sling. I set the sling on the edge of the bed and walk into the kitchen to get a drink, earbuds still in my ears. Kendrick is no longer keeping me calm, but the hook from DJ Spinall's "Ohema" guides me to glide in my socks. I open the re-frigerator door and start to pull out sandwich fixings.

There's one thing I know. I never heard anything like Afrobeat until I moved to Brooklyn. I was sitting in Darius's passenger seat watching side shows and dirt bike races while listening to E-40, Keak Da Sneak, and Mozzy. There are always the mainstream stars, folks like Lil Wayne, Drake, and Lil Rhapsody, but Darius refused to play anything that didn't allow him to "side" while he was driving. His butterscotch seats still crispy since the refurbish. He said he worked too hard to perfect his ride.

I shake my head and tear open a bag of Hal's Sweet Onion chips.

These chips go hard! And your breath goes with them but damn if it doesn't taste good! Besides, I can't sneak any Hot Cheetos in the house under Unc's rules. So, if I have a taste for sour pickles and Hot Cheetos, I got to get it on my own, on the way home from school. Even though it's real hard to find sour pickles at most of these Brooklyn bodegas.

I take my pepper turkey and cheddar cheese on a roll, my leftover cherry cheesecake, and move into the living room. I sit down with today's Revolutionary Lit class homework. We were assigned to read Toni Morrison's *The Bluest Eye* and I have to catch up with a week's worth of reading (and I want to make sure I can keep up with tomorrow's discussion).

I'm flipping through a couple of pages when the story reminds me of home. The prejudice. The pain of hating the skin you are in. The abuse that goes ignored. Being a girl is hard enough. I sit at the edge of the coffee table, my right hand naturally in my lap, and read with a highlighter in my left hand. Alternating between highlighting and picking up my sandwich. I can't put the book down.

By the time I get to chapter five, my sandwich, my cheesecake, and the sun are gone. I don't realize I am squinting until Uncle Spence walks into the house loudly. "You ain't got no lights on in here?" He flips the switch on the wall.

Friday: Bookmarks Part I

Before three days ago, I had never read a book by Toni Morrison. I mean. I know I heard of her 'cause Elena used to watch reruns on Oprah's network. But I didn't think she was writing about things that mattered to me. I read the entire book in two days. TWO DAYS! I couldn't help it. And couldn't wait to get to school to talk to Eva about the book.

I walk in with my ID ready for inspection. The security guard, Officer Tyson, nods with barely a glance. I walk past Mrs. B's office and see her reflection; I raise my left hand to catch her attention. She waves me in. "Hi, Angel, how's it going?" She smiles as I open the heavy door.

"I'm good, Mrs. B," I offer. "Just headed to Advisory."

"You're early, huh?" She is pleased.

"Yeah, I wanted to check out her library before class started. I've already finished a book and wonder if she has some other ideas of who I should read."

"You know my favorite author is Agatha Christie!" She claps her hands together. "Can't nobody write a mystery like Ms. Christie!" she exclaims.

And I chuckle. "See you at fourth period!"

"Good," she calls over her shoulder. "I've got some meeting materials I need you to collate."

I work the copy machine like a professional. It's the most I can do with my one good arm. I'll be happy when this damn sling is off. I walk into Ms. G's room. She is sitting with Ju Ju, her face frowning and serious. Ms. G is talking library low, but when she sees me she raises her voice and says, "Give me five more minutes, okay, Angel?"

"Sorry to interrupt. No problem." I back out of the room. Close the door as quietly as I can and sit on the cold tile, opposite the door, out of the way of foot traffic. I can't tell what is happening, but the tension is thick in that room. Classes still have half an hour before the bell signals the beginning of first period so the hallways are still empty. I plug my earbuds in and scroll until I find JiggyStax's page. I click the playlist titled *SundaySlumday*. I've heard it before. But it's already one of my favorites. It starts off with a track screwed and slowed down to manipulate the honey sweet of Erykah Badu's voice. Her croon slides against the bass line like a slow, slow faucet drip. I double-click the home button and search IG for JiggyStax's profile. I hate those pages with only selfies. I mean, I'm here for loving yourself but there are only so many different variations of sun in face, squat pose, and tongue-wagging selfies I can take.

JiggyStax has an interesting style.

There are landscape shots of the Brooklyn Bridge and the city; there are snapshots of albums and scenes of crate digging. I double-click the location of the record store and save the location in the notes app in my phone. There is a cool plant shot of foliage with exceptional nail art pulling at the leaves. I scroll but don't like anything—I don't want to look like a stalker! I'm all the way down to a year prior when I see a flyer. I zoom in and realize it's for a DJ event in Brooklyn. It looks like it's on President Street. What? That's the same street I people-watch. It's got to be one of those hipster bars! My blood pumps fast and my heartbeat feels like it's competing in a double Dutch competition.

Ms. G's door opens, and Ju Ju rushes out, her eyes red and watery. She puts her Yankees fitted on real low, on top of her cornrows, walks back toward the security desk and out the front door. I'm watching her leave when Ms. G opens the door firmly, then fixes the back with the colored string at the top attached to the silver screw affixed to the wall.

"Come on in, Angel. Sorry about that. You're here early?" Ms. G isn't formal. Her accent just makes her sound professional. She sits at her desk. A green flag with a red circle, green stars, and a bird perched on top of a yellow, black, and white cross is hanging on the wall behind her. I try to figure out what country it represents. I tilt my head a little to the left. She smiles. "It's a flag from my country, Dominica. The yellow represents the original people, black represents the fertile soil, and white indicates the pure water of my land. The centered stars symbolize the ten island parishes. Have you heard of Dominica before?" she asks. I shake my head. "It's a beautiful, beautiful island in the Caribbean right in the middle of Guadeloupe and Martinique." She sings, her accent dancing with delight and pride. "Anyway, how can I help?"

"Um, I had to read *The Bluest Eye* and I finished it hella fast." I tuck my earbuds into my jacket and sit my backpack on a chair near her desk.

"Wow, you must've liked it!" She leans forward.

"I did. I did. I'm wondering if you know of any other books like this?"

She's already humming and looking at the milk crate shelves behind her. "Oh, Angel, you've come to the perfect place." And I think Ms. G squeals! I giggle. "Don't mind me." She's searching through the crates. "I just work at a bookstore part-time because I need the discounts. I buy more books than a teacher's salary can afford! And I'm even part of a book club for women of color. The Well-Read Black Girl! We meet every month at a local women's cooperative space."

She is stacking books and talking hurriedly. Like there is a prize attached to each book she pulls from the crate before she finally turns back to face me and reveals the stack of books.

I gasp. "Oh no!" Now I'm afraid. It's like she turned into a book monster. But it's sweet Ms. G.

"Oh, stop it!" She cackles. "Inside each of these books is an index card describing the kind of book that it is, using music icons as a compass. I'll read them to you, and you get to choose which one sounds the best!"

"Whew," I half joke.

"Now, these books are their own special sauce. Toni Morrison is iconic. She is exceptional. But each of these authors has a quality of literary excellence too. The trick is that you want to find your circle of writers. You get to decide what kind of storyteller you like, then you explore the genre. By the time you've done that—you'll be excited to try new genres. Yes?" She peers at me as she places each book gingerly on her desk.

"Yes," I answer because she stops mid-placement to look me in my eyes and make sure I'm listening.

"Good," she chirps. She picks up one book with a green-and-red cover, opens the flap, and pulls out a bright yellow index card. "First, this is Sandra Cisneros's *The House on Mango Street*. Think soulful poetics of H.E.R. and essence of Celia Cruz with the details of a neighborhood so perfect and sprawling you can taste it! It's in vignettes—"

"What's that?" I ask.

She looks up from her script. "Vignettes are like small short stories. Like episodes of a television show?" I nod. "This is all about a girl growing up in Chicago. It talks about social class issues, gender roles, and family." She returns the index card to the inside crease of the cover, and the green book with a red building on the front is closed.

I had no idea my whole life was a series of vignettes.

I remember the day Amir was brought home. In a cream-colored blanket and a blue cap.

I was with Uncle Spence waiting for the old, gray, two-door Cutlass to park in the garage. I was so excited to welcome my little brother I squealed. My dad smacked my mouth closed with his rough sandpaper hands.

"Be quiet before you scare the baby to death."

My hand over my mouth and the tears blurring my eyes. I think he hushed me for good. Uncle Spence said I didn't speak for another three weeks.

Her hands move over to a brown book with a woman's face sketched in black. The woman's eyes are closed, her right shoulder naked and exposed. "Now this is Zora Neale Hurston, ahead of her time! No one really liked this book when it first came out—but it's so good! Actually, this was turned into a film too, with Halle Berry and what's his name—he has eyes like yours?" I shrug. A lot of people have eyes like mine. "Never mind," she continues, and pulls out a hot-pink index card. "This book, *Their Eyes Were Watching God,* is Frank Ocean meets Gary Clark Jr. There is a deep sorrow to this book. There is a slow crawl through Florida scenery, dealing with the effects of slavery, and a woman being treated like a voiceless trophy wife because she is a Black woman with light skin. This story unravels her journey as she searches for love and finds it in an unlikely character. The love story is breathtaking." I roll my eyes.

She smiles tightly and returns it to the desktop. "Okay," she sings, grabbing a red book and pulling out a red index card. "This is Maya Angelou. She's an amazing poet who performed the inaugural poem for—"

"Yes, I know her!" I'm excited to know the right answer, finally! My fingertips are buzzing. I rub my elbow and feel the extra energy scuttle through the room. I look at the red book. On the cover is a bright yellow sun and a black bird flying up.

"Great! *I Know Why the Caged Bird Sings* is a collection of personal essays. Now, while they are autobiographical, they are still poetic and drawl through many beautiful stories of her coming into her own. We get to witness her story from childhood to marriage. Think the ethereal sound of James Blake meets the sweet, sad tide of Billie Holiday!"

Rewind: Oma

I had no idea my whole life was a series of vignettes quilted together into some kind of life.

The first time I knew sadness had a name I watched Elena and my dad fight. She was in the kitchen, I think. It was Christmas break, I think. Amir and I played with our toys near the door, I think. She screamed, I think. We ran outside, I think. Amir cried, I think. The sky was still opening for the high sun's arrival.

But we ran, I remember now.

Our matching pajamas, with Disney characters dancing on our chests, as we raced next door to call our oma. Her voice sang after the second ring, *Merry Christmas.* And my voice didn't sing because my heart was beating too fast.

"Oma! She's on the kitchen floor. He hit her," I croaked.

Her voice turned from tinsel and glitter to hot stone. "Here I come. Don't move."

I nod as Ms. G places the card back into the book and grabs another red book.

"This is Sapphire's *Push,* think the gut punch 'never know what's next' of Cardi B with some drama of Beyoncé's *Lemonade.* It's discussing abuse and the obstacles a young teen mom will survive to reclaim her own joy. Some of it reads like prose." When I squint my eyes, she explains, "Which is like long lines of poetry. It's an intense story. But it's one of the most honest accounts of a girl's survival."

She picks up the last book. It's teal green with a white dog on the cover. The pages are upturned and there is a gold star on it. Inside is a gold-yellow notecard. She clears her throat. "This is Jesmyn Ward's *Salvage the Bones.* Think the beautiful tone of Nina Simone and the spitfire choir of Lauryn Hill. Now think of those two mavens meeting for tea in Louisiana." She claps her hands, pleased. "The story takes place a couple of days before and after Hurricane Katrina through the narrative of a fifteen-year-old girl." I nod again. "This is one of my favorite books of all time. The story has siblings and pets and family and fear. It has everything." Ms. G takes a step back and braces herself. Places the last index card back in the book and marvels at the selection on her desk. "Now. Which one would you like to borrow?"

I look between the selections one more time, then look at Ms. G. "I think I'll try the one with the dog."

The Period Bell Can Sound Like an Emergency Bell If You Aren't Paying Attention

Eva's not in school today. Mrs. B said something about a youth leadership conference in Washington, D.C., but I'm excited to finish this new book from Ms. G. I walk to the cafeteria and grab a seat near the door. I pull out a KIND bar and a small bag of carrots and an apple. I'm searching my backpack with one pod in my ear when I hear two dudes joke to each other loudly. "Yo, look at Shorty with the broke arm. I'd definitely smash." My body goes cold. Eyes hot daggers and fist clench ready. It isn't as though I've never heard the words before. It's just that I don't think I was prepared. My hands fumble with the dog-eared book and I drop it on the table and glare up. "Oh shit! Look at her eyes. Yo, Ma, you got them cat eyes, like Badu!" A short, wide-sized kid with a football and backpack begins to walk my way.

"Come on, Biz," a voice calls from over my shoulder. "Go on with that, kid. She's Kamilah's friend." Biz, the foulmouthed one, almost drops his football as he stops in his tracks. I lift my eyebrows, surprised. Biz walks away, back toward the lunch line, before I follow the voice. It's Sterling.

"Hey." He's wearing the same ash-gray hoodie and red tracksuit pants.

"Hey, Angel," he responds. "Kamilah told me to look out for you."

My mouth falls open. Surprised. After we saw each other at the park, I thought I left too hastily. I blamed myself and all my feelings the entire walk home.

"I appreciate that." I pick up the book and place it safely in my backpack along with my snacks. "But I don't need your help. I can take care of myself." I move past Sterling, his mouth open like a door, and head to the library to find a dark corner to hide in.

During the last H.E.R. Leadership Advisory, we go around the circle and describe our mood using the number system, and then name one thing we are thankful for. Eva says, "Privacy." Ju Ju says, "Swag." RaChelle says, "Forgiveness." Kamilah says, "Avion." Teiya says, "Silence." And I am so emotional, I almost cry before catching my breath. "This," I say after a couple of uninterrupted seconds. I had just finished Toni Morrison's book. So, I really think I was in my feelings. Kamilah hands me a Kleenex without missing a beat. And Reina comes in right after. "I'm grateful for my friends, yo. And Brooklyn. We always got Brooklyn."

Ms. G moves on pretty quickly after that. But Kamilah just stares at me and mouths, "You okay?" I nod. Pull the hood over my head and steel myself for the rest of the day. After finishing *The Bluest Eye,* my heart is heavy, like I got a bunch of stones in my pocket.

Books make you tap into your own memories. Those memories come with old feelings—feelings you think you've put to bed. Just to find out after each page is read and the story unfolds, those memories have awakened, one by one. Memories of being afraid. Memories of being not enough. Memories of being misjudged. The kind of things that keep you up at night. Or the kind of things that make you want to flip into survival mode when someone randomly catcalls you.

Have You Ever Been Catcalled?

It's like running running running

Forever

Toward safety

Away from the sounds that scare you most

It's like pretending you are in control

of your own life

of your own ideas

with no idea

of who wants to take your light from you

It's like running

Until you hit a wall

And the wall doesn't budge

And the wall doesn't care that you're scared

And you've been taught to fear the sound of walls

blocking your path

blocking your way

blocking your vision

Have you ever been catcalled?

Been called

Ma

Sweetie

Sugar

Honey

By people who don't know you

They sound so sweet when they say

Sweetie

Sugar

Ma

   Yo!   Ma!

Your heart knows you can't trust it

And your blood races

And your eyes dart

And you begin to sweat

Because you've seen what those sweet nothings can become

If you don't accept them gracefully

If you don't acknowledge them

Have you ever been catcalled?

And witnessed Ma transform into the word BITCH

And watched Baby bloom, then cut into the word SLUT

And learned how easily Sugar can be shortened into a nasty slur

Have you ever been catcalled?

Have you ever been chased?

Have you ever been followed?

Have you ever had to run, swing & hide from danger?

Have you ever been followed?

Have you ever been chased?

    Up the block?

    Behind the stairs?

    Have you felt your heart beat beat beating

    in your chest?

    Have you felt your heart beat stutter step kick and climb

    its way up your throat?

Have you ever been bitten for saying, No thank you?

Have you ever been kicked for saying, I'm not interested?

Have you ever felt like you might not make it home safe?

Have you ever felt like you might not make it home?

Have you ever felt like you might not make it?

Botanical Brooklyn

Uncle Spence wants to get out of the house early. He has the weekend off for the next couple of months to make sure I'm not alone. He exclaims: *You know how many favors I owe to get a month of Saturdays free?* And this is our first Saturday out together. When I first moved here, I was holed up in the closet/room. I didn't go to school. And I didn't think I would make it another day. I had no phone privileges. And I was under constant watch. Uncle said he wanted to make sure I was okay. I think he was afraid I would hurt myself. I can't lie, I was afraid too.

I arrived in the John F. Kennedy Airport looking like a shell of myself. I was too numb to argue with anyone anymore and only spoke with head nods and short answers. Yes or no. Nothing more. Uncle Spence had never seen me like that. Out of touch, I heard him say on the phone once. The airport employee wheeled me to the baggage claim in a wheelchair, and it felt like that one scene from the Spike Lee film about Malcolm X, where the world is moving around Malcolm and he's just sitting there—waiting for the world to slow down a little.

As soon as the double doors of baggage claim opened up, and Uncle saw I had a black eye and a medical sling, he started to cry. After that moment, with people looking at my uncle cry at my feet and me, not being able to really do anything except look at him sadly, I didn't feel like moving anywhere past the apartment's front door. We live in a five-story walk-up. Sure, there is an elevator for the elderly. But it is so slow and compact, folks only seem to use it for emergencies or when they have too many bags of groceries to maneuver upstairs alone.

At first, I only walked around the neighborhood with Uncle as my chaperone. And when Uncle went to work, I closed myself up in my small room. Elena calls every few days. She hasn't missed a weekend to check in, but I still have nothing to say to her. I was mad when she forced me to come to Brooklyn. "Borough of Kings," she said. But I'm still mad, even if after all these weeks, it's beginning to feel like I belong.

I miss my Amir. Whenever Amir calls, I scramble to Uncle Spence's side, to hear what he has to say.

"I got the scholarship for boarding school!" he shrieks. His voice still childlike. And I am so happy for him I start to cry. "Don't cry, Angel. We are all going to be okay," he promises. "The triplets are staying with their Nana Henry. And I'm going to live on campus. My counselor just told me a space opened. And Ma promises to visit me once a month! We're okay. It's all going to be fine. Take care of yourself. You get to live in a whole new world! And it's up to you to take it all in." He sounds like Uncle Spence, all motivational and stuff. But he keeps going. "We're okay. We're okay. We're okay," he chants until my tears dry.

After talking to Amir, I feel a little bit more like myself. I walk out the burgundy-painted steel door of our apartment and down the parkway by myself. I don't know where I am going. But I let my legs lead me toward the busy sounds of the intersection. I cross the street and a woman dressed in an African-print skirt is passing out business cards. Usually, I have my earbuds in and I just nod and pass, but this time I take a glossy print.

She offers: "Braid your hair, sis? We give you a student discount." I stop walking. Look at the yellow-and-red awning with pictures of different braided hairstyles covering the glass. Pictures of different brown faces with box braids, high ponytail cornrow with a waterfall of braids, invisible braids, boho locs, so many hairstyles with beads or bangs or both.

"Can you take me now?" I ask.

"Yes, come inside. Look at the book and pick the style you like most."

Sunday Brunch Day

Uncle Spence treats me to brunch at Cheryl's Global Soul. It's a neighborhood eatery owned by a Black woman with beautiful, brown, long dreadlocks. Her peppered thick ropes of hair swish against the middle of her back when she walks by, sounding out a song of its own. Her eyes are smiling when she sees us. "Hey, Spence!" He goes to talk to her briefly. Their laughter spills over the coffee counter before we're seated beneath a heater and a painting of a woman with a gardenia crown. I order the kids' special: *Silver Dollar Pancakes with Bananas and a side of Vanilla Ice Cream!* I run my hand over my freshly cornrowed hair, careful not to mess up the pro-styled, gelled-down baby hairs. Uncle orders the Kenny, which turns out to be a fried fish sandwich with a salad and fries.

"Oh, we can share!" I laugh.

"Nah. You got to get your own, niece," he responds. And orders an additional side of French fries before handing back his menu.

"How's school going?" he asks, picking up his coffee mug. "I see you walking around with all these books lately." Uncle's right. After I finished *Salvage the Bones* on Saturday, I went to the library and checked out *Brown Girl Dreaming*. I remember the cover from Ms. G's collection. It's been only two days and I can't bear to put the book down. Woodson wrote: "When there are many worlds you can choose the one you walk into each day." I can't stop thinking about that quote.

"I guess I kind of lose myself in them," I murmur before my attention turns to the waitress in tight jeans walking toward our table holding a tin cup overflowing with shoestring fries. "Thank you," we say in unison.

Uncle Spence's phone vibrates, and I think, *Here we go . . . back to work.* I grab a handful of hot French fries as the waitress nods and smiles quickly before moving to the next table to fill the emptying cups of an arguing couple. A woman wearing various pink to magenta swatches and perfect-pout pink lip gloss doesn't notice the refill. And her partner's eyes are fixed on her pretty, stony face, but her fingers are dancing on top of the handle of her coffee cup. The waitress breaks the spell, and they release their intense eye contact. They thank her for the refill before looking back into each other's eyes. The one still holding tight on their coffee cup is dressed in a long brown tunic and leather boots. They reach over the table and squeeze the fingers of the woman with the magenta makeup; her thick black mascara is beginning to run south. Her eyes flutter open and closed. I can't look away. Coffee Handle Bae lightly dabs her tearstains with a white fabric napkin in her other hand. Her free hand grabs his and tightens. They hold one another with interlocked fingers. I look away, embarrassed by how nosy I am. Surprised at the warmth settling in my stomach, I reach for the book tucked in my backpack.

Uncle Spence puts his phone away with a frown.

"You okay?" I ask him.

"Nah," he responds honestly. Uncle is always honest. He never says niceties to lessen the blow with the truth. He says it takes too much time.

I have never really known anything like it. Back home, adults lie to their children all the time. Lies about, "Why are you crying?" Lies about, "Why can't we go over to that house?" Lies about, "Who are you really?" Lies on lies on lies.

For so long, I was looking for the truth from people that I let their words speak when their actions were louder. Now I believe people for who they show me they are. Until they prove they are someone else.

Words are easy to fake. But actions tell you everything you need to know about a person.

"I have to go in for a shift. Someone called out sick and there are no other techs available. But I still have a couple of hours. I'm sorry. I wanted to hang out with you today. Take you to Albee Square for some real fall-style clothes, show you some murals around the neighborhood. Take you by the farmer's market to get a couple of things, because you can't eat bodega sandwiches every day."

"No, Unc, YOU can't eat them every day." I laugh. "I definitely can."

"You want to—but that can't happen?" He sips his coffee. "How about we walk by the farmer's market, it's right at the arch by Grand Army Plaza, and then you make your way to Albee Square to get a couple of things on your own? We can check out the Biggie and Sean P murals next weekend?" Our plates arrive and I'm already pouring syrup on my kid-sized banana-covered pancakes.

I nod in agreement.

"Good." He sighs. "You need a pair of Timbs too." He takes a huge bite into his sandwich, the basil mayo falling on the plate. All the colors begin to look like the beginning of a Basquiat painting. I look up quizzically. He explains after a gulp. "Winter is coming," he jokes. His *Game of Thrones* reference tickles him. I shake my head and take another bite.

I haven't seen *GoT*, but Amir told me all about it. He read all the books. Honestly, I was intimidated by the dictionary-sized books! (He'd be so proud of me right now! Look at me, I'm the kind of girl that carries a book in her backpack.) Besides, I'm not really into the fairy tale about dragons and white-haired ladies who free slaves. But I do have a lot of respect for Amir's favorite character: Arya. The little assassin sister? A girl standing up for herself and her family, yeah, she sounds lit.

Text Message I

ANGEL

TBH I'm like Arya in this library.

How's campus? How are The Trio?

AMIR

ROFL Arya in library?

What are you talking about?

Asha, Ashanti and Ayanna are at their pops right now.

Mom picked up some work at the stadium

Campus is so green, Angel.

It's like sculptures and green grass everywhere.

That sounds so cool. I'm so proud of you, Amir. I wish I could be there to see you in one of those fancy ties.

You okay?

I think so. I miss you guys. That's all.

Mom says she hasn't talked to you yet.

. . .

Don't be so hard on Mom.

She's trying. I'll text you later.

I got study group in an hour. ILY, big sis

LYM little big brother

Grand Army Plaza

Me and Uncle Spence walk to the farmer's market two blocks over and shop for a couple of things. We walk by different vendors, grabbing a bag of apples, a bunch of bananas, bell peppers, red onions, potatoes, and stalks of broccoli. We finish our shopping and Uncle walks me to the Grand Army Plaza subway station so I can head to the mall and buy some clothes. He hands me his credit card. And before I can grab it, he snatches it back. "Be careful. Do not lose this card. Do not over-spend. This ain't no Richie Rich shit."

I nod. I'm pretty responsible with things like this. I mean, I'm used to buying everything from the thrift store, minus underwear and bras. My Converse were a birthday present that I've kept clean for two years. (You should see the magic I am capable of with a toothbrush and a dirty shoe!) But when you are the oldest of five and your little brother is taller and skinnier than you, you deal with it. So out-of-season polo tees and ripped jeans with old hoodies just became my uniform. Sure, I want J's. And when I got them as a gift from Darius, I was so in awe that I was afraid to wear them. And when we fell out—I left them Nikes at the hospital ER.

Uncle Spence hands me the credit card again and I tuck it into my back pocket with my free hand. His eyes go dark.

"Last weekend with that thing, huh? How you feel?"

"Good, I guess. I've been doing the exercises on my own. We'll see what Dr. Patterson says on Monday."

He tries to hide his interest. "After school, right? If you meet me, I'll walk you over to Scottie's office."

I smirk. Scottie Patterson isn't pretty. She's gorgeous. Like she's a triple threat: stylish, smart, and a doctor. She has this fire-red hair that she wears in a low bun and a soda-bottle figure that she hides beneath her white lab coat. She sings Biggie lyrics when walking the halls at the hospital where both she and Uncle work. She's the only one that calls Uncle *Tech T.* It's so cute. When I first met her, she beatboxed then sang his name as soon as she saw him. He pretends he doesn't like her like *that* that, but he does. I can tell.

"Whatever, yo." He doesn't even argue. He just walks away.

"I'll see you later," I sing to him as he flips his leather coat collar up to his ears and shifts the grocery bag's weight from his left to his right.

"You just hit me when you get home," he calls over his shoulder. And I could swear I hear his voice almost bubble over with laughter.

Uncle & Scottie

The way Uncle's face lights up at the sound of her name

Reminds me of the way Mom and Pops used to look at one another

After Amir was born, there was no more pretending sleep to watch

Them dance in each other's arms

There were only arguments and fighting and yelling and crying

But the way Uncle's face lights up at the sound of Scottie's name

Makes me think love can happen

And be a safe place to rest

Love can make people laugh

Love can do more than make people cry

Love is my uncle's eyes swaying to the sound of possibilities

Even if he won't admit it

Yet

Albee Square Mall

I climb out of the subway station and look for the McDonald's intersection. It's not called that, it's just the burger spot where all the kids from Brooklyn Tech and some kids from Banneker High hang out after last bell rings. Albee Square Mall is also my landmark to make sure I walk in the right direction when heading to Fulton Street. It's easy—McDonald's, Junior's, Manhattan Bridge equals right direction. Brooklyn Academy of Music, Barclays Center, Prospect Park equals wrong direction. I had to figure this out quick. There is nothing worse than walking for ten minutes before you get smacked by all the wind and realize you've been going the wrong way the entire time.

I take a left on Fulton Street and pass the cell phone store, beauty supply store, and bank. There is a large hole in the ground surrounded by a wooden gate of ultramarine-blue boards, a sign that they demolished another building. I peek through a jagged opening of the rickety blue board. I see: there is a rusty yellow dump truck sitting full of dirt covered by a dark green tarp. People walk around me, unbothered or concerned. I move away slowly and ignore the signs of a city being crushed into a new version of itself. Just like home.

My uncle loves this part of Brooklyn and loves to remind me of Biz Markie's "Albee Square Mall" song by singing up the hallway on the way to the bathroom: Go shoppin' / Go shoppin' / Go shoppin' / Let's all go shoppin'.

He said, "I was here every chance I got. If I wasn't working at the hospital, I was at Beat Street, waiting to see who was coming in and out the store. This is the joint Jay-Z rapped about! This is the place Biz and Kane and Tribe and Rakim and all the greats visited. This is where hip-hop lived!"

Walking down the Albee Square Mall today, one might think that hip-hop lived in a clothing store geared toward the business-casual savvy office assistant. Walking down the street today, no one would know the basement of this building was once the home of the hip-hop gem. Where my uncle, a young twenty-two-year-old, fresh off a sixteen-hour shift, still wearing his scrubs and a worn pair of Air Max, would wait outside with copies of a mixtape he made when he wasn't sleeping or working. My uncle Spence would play the mixtape in the break room and have his friends walking around singing his newest mix. My uncle Spence, so buzzed from the high of loving music and his new career, would live on that buzz and go to the basement record store for new vinyl drops and possible MC sightings. He wanted to share his mixtape. Maybe move one of them so much they would give him a drop for his next mixtape.

Mixtapes were a big deal back in the early 2000s. They were sold cheap and on plastic card tables up and down streets like Jamaica Avenue in Queens, Malcolm X Boulevard in Harlem, Canal Street in Manhattan, the Grand Concourse in the Bronx, and up and down Brooklyn's Albee Square Mall, featuring different images of hip-hop moguls and Bad Boy MCs on the cover with gold and silver blinged lettering and girls in bikinis or booty shorts on the back of motorcycles, their middle fingers held high in the sky. Usually, a DJ's name was graffiti-blocked with their tag line near the list of song titles protecting the flimsy shiny music disc.

Rewind: Mixtapes

When I first arrived to the small second room of Uncle Spence's apartment, I found a bunch of these CD covers in an empty drawer in my bedroom/closet. The drawer was filled with old flyers, letters splashed across the top in red, black, and green: DJ Tech T. I asked Uncle what to do with them, he grabbed them quickly and said, *Sorry about that. I'll handle it.* Uncle took the entire drawer out from the frame and retreated to his room.

I knew he had a love for music. Elena said he used to hoard records in the family garage, keeping them in milk crates against the entire wall. While everyone was at school or work, the family house over on Twenty-Fourth Street suspiciously caught fire. The mountain of molten records burned for days. Elena said, *You could smell the reek of despair in the air. Something in my little brother broke that day.*

Years later, after graduating from high school and then community college, Uncle Spence left for the East Coast to live on his own. He told the family he needed to leave and focused on becoming an X-ray technician. He was too wrapped up running errands and being taken for granted as the youngest. He also was tired of Elena's first boyfriend, Ray. My dad. He kept finding himself in the middle of two grown-ups fighting. No one wanted to get in the middle of it.

One night, after the police escorted Elena and Ray from their shared bedroom in an apartment complex, Uncle sat with his flip phone on his lap, broken in half as a result of breaking up a fight. It was two days after his twentieth birthday. He loved his big sister, Elena, and he only wanted her to be happy and safe. Uncle Spence asked her to leave town with him. Said, *I found a program and am headed to the East Coast for work. I'll take care of us. Just come with me. This is dangerous. This won't work.*

Elena was sitting on the concrete stair of the parking lot, her face wet with tears. She wiped her face and flicked her lighter awake. *I can't leave Ray,* she said. *He's the only man that ever loved me.* This is when Uncle realized, *It's time for me to follow my own dreams.*

It wasn't until I found those mixtape sleeves and old flyers that I began to realize how being a DJ was such a large part of Uncle Spence's dreams. Uncle returned to the room a while later and placed the empty drawer back to store my personal items in. I asked him again about its previous contents. But he just shrugged and said, "DJ Tech T, that was a long time ago."

Later that night I lay looking at cracks in the ceiling. They stretch from the far corner of the room all the way to the window. I unfold the slip of paper with "DJ Tech T" in thick script, on the top, from its safe place in the small carriage of my backpack near the foot of the bed. I sit here looking at it, using the moon as my night-light, my fingers following the creases of the page like I am trying to read my own future.

Inside the shoe store, the staff are wearing referee uniforms and bright-colored sneakers. "Hello, how you doing today? Let us know if you need anything!" a cheery voice sings from behind the cash register as a girl with blond-tipped dreads scans a stack of shoeboxes.

I nod, replace the earbuds, and turn up DJ JiggyStax's latest mix. This morning I downloaded the newest mix and am excited to hear what waits for me. Listening to music is more than calming—it feels like a recharge. JiggyStax's manipulation of sound guides me through my search for my first pair of Timberland boots and this new life. When I am listening to music, it makes the hardest task seem possible.

I pick up a pair of all-black Timberland boots and they are so heavy I almost drop them! I never had a reason to wear a pair of construction boots. In California, flip-flops, Vans, and Chucks were just fine. I turn them over to look for the price when I feel a tap on my shoulder. I turn around with the boot still in hand before I lose my grip.

Sterling is standing in front of me, referee shirt tucked into black pants and wearing a pair of red-and-white checkered Vans. He leans over to pick up the boot and I yank the earbuds out of my ears, embarrassed by my clumsiness.

"Damn! Sorry! I mean, hey?!"

Sterling is still bending over, laughing as he stands upright, and I feel my face burning. "You okay?"

He places the boot in its rightful place. "I didn't mean to scare you." His shoulders are still shaking. And I feel my right hand begin to tingle. *Must be my circulation,* I think.

"You didn't scare me," I correct him. "You just surprised me."

"I asked what you were looking for." His eyes don't look so sad today. "But I don't think you heard me." He picks up a dangling earbud tangled in the string of my hoodie.

Wow. My heart flips and I pull away from his attention. From his closeness. It isn't that I'm frightened. I just haven't been able to feel anything but anger. I mean, not until now. My cheeks deepen in warmth and I look up at him defiantly. "I didn't hear you. I was into this new mix."

"Word? Who you listening to?" He steps back and begins to scour the racks of shoes before he straightens out a column of shelves until all the shoes are in neat and perfect rows.

"Oh, just a DJ on SoundCloud." I reach for the black Timberland boots again.

"Oh, ight." He smiles and crosses his hands.

"What?" I ask, the heavy boot still in the palm of my good hand.

"Are these your first pair of Timbs?" he asks, and I nod. He reaches for the boot in my hand. "Then you don't want these." He replaces them on the stand and reaches behind me for a tan boot. "Black Timbs look good. But you need the classic joints first. What size are you, an eight?" I nod again, but now in shock. "Bet. This is an eight right here. Try this one on," he instructs, pointing to a cushion seat behind me. "Now these," he says in a game show host voice, "unlike the Mac and Cheese Timbs, which are fresh; or the beef and broccoli, which are lit"—he points to a row of different boots. They line the shelf like shoe candy—"these are the originals. They are a New York staple and match almost everything. These should be your first pair." He loosens the strings and puts the boot near my socked foot. I've already pulled my shoe off and am about to stuff my foot in the boot when he brushes my hand. I don't want to be corny. But I definitely felt something. Electricity?

Sterling pretends he doesn't notice. He jumps up and says, almost out of breath, "I'll be right back. Let me get the other shoe."

I watch him leave behind a thick black curtain before I shake my head to clear the thoughts beginning to form. "Nah," I say out loud. "Nope." And I push the lone boot aside to put my sneaker back on. I pick the boot up and walk to the cash register.

"Did anyone help you today?" the girl with the cheery voice calls from the register.

"Yeah, Sterling helped me," I reply. "He went to get the other shoe. I'll get these."

"Sterling!" She calls behind the curtain, "Hurry up." He reappears and so do the clouds in my head.

"Thanks, Sterling." I busy myself with finding Uncle's credit card to ignore Sterling's stare. He's standing six inches taller than the girl with blond dreads and his hands are in his pockets. I pull the card out and hand it over with a tiny smile.

He's still looking at me.

"No problem. Give her my discount, Keke." He smiles before his face darkens. "What's up, Biz?"

"Yo! What's good, Sterling? Oh snap! Whaddup, Angel Eyes?" Biz is walking into the store, loud and boisterous, taking up more space than there is door. It isn't his size; it's his energy.

I don't respond. I don't like Biz. So I won't pretend to.

"Will that be all?" Keke asks as she tosses her mane to the side. She waves her hand like a commercial for manicures and adds, "We have 'buy one bundle of socks, get one free' if you're interested?"

I shake my head no, my eyes still on Sterling. My back is hot from where I feel Biz staring.

"Oh, ight, Angel," Biz interrupts dramatically. "I see how it is."

Keke and I both ignore Biz. "They're perfect for these boots," she adds.

"I think I'm good, thank you, though," I direct to Keke.

Biz huffs.

My jaw sets to stone.

"Yo, Biz! Check these out." Sterling moves from behind the cash register and daps Biz's fist as they walk to the other side of the store.

Keke rolls her eyes and smiles at me. "Girl," she growls. "He needs to mind his own business." She throws both hands up, each beautifully manicured fingernail into the sky. Then swipes the card. "Sign here," she says sweetly, passing me the receipt as she bags the box of shoes.

Biz's back is toward me as I walk out. "Thank you," I mouth to Keke as I head to the door.

Sterling and I stare at each other for one more beat before the door opens, and I exit into the quick-footed music of Brooklyn.

Text Message 2

AMIR

You hear about Darius?

ANGEL

I haven't heard from him since I left.

I also have a new number. Unc wasn't having it.

They picked him up. Mom just told me.

She tried to call you and tell you.

Why won't you take her calls?

I'm not ready to talk to her. What about Darius.

They got it on video. The incident. And an incident
report from the security guard that Darius swung on.

Damn.

I know. It's wild. Mom said
they might ask you to come back and . . .

It's bad enough I can barely sleep.

I can't do this. TTYL

I'm sorry, Angel.

It's not your fault.

. . .

I'm still sorry.

Back Beneath the Blue Sky

I try to get ahold of my nerves. I take a deep breath like the meditation app suggests. I inhale and hold my breath for five seconds and exhale. I take another deep breath in, and this time I taste everything. I smell the beauty of Brooklyn: Cesar's chicken-and-cheese empanadas with tomatillo sauce; Rose Love incense burning from one of the nearby vendor tables cloaked with different wooden trinkets, a corkboard full of handmade earrings, and kente cloth; churros covered by aluminum foil balanced on a black laundry cart; steaming piles of yellow rice and chicken kebabs with peppers from the yellow halal food truck; beef and turkey sausages from the corner stand. I even smell the sugar in the orange-and-red punch bubbling in the window. My stomach growls. Even though I just ate brunch, Brooklyn has the best food, so I can always eat. But I must finish shopping, or I'll be walking back onto campus with the same black jeans and fading hoodie. I've begun to wear a hole in the sleeve from the Velcro on the shoulder sling.

"Heyyy, Angel!" I hear over my shoulder. I turn and see Eva walking toward me. She is wearing a black business jacket with blue jeans and oxblood Doc Martens. I smile at her choice of consistently fresh outfits.

"Eva!" I haven't seen her since she left to represent the school at the youth leadership conference. "You look so cute," I compliment her wide-brimmed black hat and large silver hoops.

"Thank you." She blushes, and I can't believe she's acting shy.

"You got some new kicks, huh?" She points to my bag. I nod. "Good. 'Cause when the snow hits, you don't want to be stuck out here with sneakers. Where you headed?"

"I don't know." I sigh. "I need to buy clothes for fall and my uncle was going to take me, but he had to work. So I'm figuring it out. I guess I'll check out the mall next." I shrug.

"OOH! I love to shop a little bit. You like thrifting?" And I'm shocked. I always had to pretend about where I bought my clothes before. I had never heard anyone excited about buying secondhand clothes.

"I wouldn't say I like it." I laugh a little. It's just the only thing my mom could afford, really.

She frowns. "Look, the average American will throw away over eighty pounds of clothes a year—that's almost thirty billion pounds of clothing in a landfill, and for what? To have the newest J's?" I look at her Doc Martens and lift my eyebrow.

"I bought these at the thrift, Ma. Don't get it twisted. I like nice things too. My prom dress I'm having made by Sister Keba over on Bedford Avenue, but most of this can be found in consignment, and honestly, it reduces our footprint, reduces the use of energy, and gives back to the community." She points to my bag. "Some things you just need to buy new, I get it. But fair trade and thrifting is the wave. Do you trust me?" I nod. "Then come on. I got a couple of hours before I need to head home. I got an IG Live discussion with a body image activist."

"What's a body image activist?" I ask, following her across the street.

"It's someone that fights against ideas of a beauty monolith."

I stop in my tracks. "What?"

She grabs my good arm and laughs, pulling me with her. "It means thinking there is only ONE way to be pretty. Like when little Black and brown kids only see white baby dolls. Or when bilingual people only see English speakers as supervisors and bosses. It's the constant fight for the respect of different ethnicities, cultures, and genders. You know? There isn't one way to be beautiful."

Rewind: He Used to Call Me Beautiful

I was trying on clothes in a makeshift dressing room at a thrift shop and the word *beautiful* was ringing through my head. *Beautiful.* Darius called me that. It was such a different word. It sounded so mature. I had been called cute and pretty. But no one had ever called me *beautiful* before.

The second time I met Darius was at my school basketball game. I acted like I didn't see him. He saw me pretend but wasn't fazed. He simply called me over, asked me to sit beside him, while all the girls from my school gawked. *Jealous?* I thought. They were usually so quick to call me names and spread lies about me that I was fine sitting next to Darius when he asked. Because he asked. And because he didn't care about people or what they thought.

People were afraid of Darius. But I wasn't. I saw a different side of him that day at the mall. He was kind and considerate, opening the door for me and walking me all the way to the storefront entrance. I didn't really want to be with these girls, taking pictures that would be given away to scrutinize and joke about later. But I was trying to get outside of my head and show a different side of myself.

That's what Elena suggested. She had a day off, which rarely happened, and she was on her way to get the triplets from their dad's house. I was pouting on the couch and fuming.

"I have nothing to wear. These people hate me. You should hear what they say about you!"

Elena shrugged and said, "People been talking about me my whole life, and what did it get me?"

Darius didn't care what people said. He didn't cower or play quiet.

When I sat by him on the bleachers, my back straight, my eyes looking directly into his, he said, "You are so beautiful."

After that, I didn't leave his side. I decided if he could tell me that so easily, so simply, then maybe, just maybe, I wouldn't feel so alone.

Sure, it might not have been healthy. Being together all the time. And Amir didn't like him. Which is funny, because Amir is easygoing. But when he learned Darius wanted the password to my Instagram and Darius checked my messages on my phone, he stopped talking to Darius altogether. The night before the incident, the horn honked from outside our front door. I turned to rush out when Amir grabbed my right hand and said, "Don't go, Ang."

But Amir never knew what it was like to be me. Everyone loved him. Everyone has always loved him. Especially me. And for the first time, I had someone looking out for me. The same way I looked out for Amir, Ayanna, Asha, and Ashanti. Elena's parents were both dead. And Uncle Spence lived in Brooklyn. Elena worked long hours to make ends meet and to afford Amir's tuition; and the triplets' dad's family didn't want us around.

I began to think Darius was all I had. And he bought me things I'd never had the money to buy before, so I figured the attention was love. That's what I said when we argued over stupid things. But love can't be bought, and love doesn't hurt. I thought being with him would make me less lonely.

I was wrong.

It's Almost Two Months Since the Incident and I See Things Different Now

I try on a camouflage jacket, turn around in the mirror, and tilt my head. It swallows my whole body. I didn't realize how much weight I had lost. I haven't taken pictures or posted. I haven't checked email and I have a new phone number.

Uncle said I had to start fresh. Elena doesn't even have the number. She calls Uncle to talk to me. But I don't have nothing to say. When he tries to hand me the phone, I find a way to be in the bathroom and yell in response to his constant door knocking, "Privacy!" It's not that I'm mad. I think I'm just too numb.

I try on a jean jacket. It fits much better. It's big enough to put a sweater beneath it but fitted enough to feel like I can dress it up. It has "Blessed" on the back of it with three stripes. I smile.

"You okay in there?" Eva calls from the dressing room lobby. Which was just a fancy way of saying the other side of the green suede curtain.

"Yeah. I like the jeans but not the camouflage. And these jeans don't fit. They're too tight," I say, trying to pull up a pair of deep blue jeans.

"How about this?" She pushes her hand through a crack in the curtain. She's holding a pair of vintage acid-wash jeans and a snakeskin lime cropped puff coat.

I gasp. "Oh, I love these! My mom used to have on a pair like these in this old Polaroid picture I found!" I start giggling as I struggle to take off the too-tight pair and pull on the new pair without hurting my arm. As I gather them and gingerly close the button, I am so excited they fit. I open the curtain still wearing the jean jacket and now a pair of pants that fit. My arm is naked of its usual shoulder sling, but I figure in twenty-four hours it will be off for good—*I'll be careful.*

"What do you think?" I ask under Eva's appraising eyes.

"Oh my goodness—you don't have on the sling! Are you okay?"

I nod emphatically.

"Angel, you look beautiful!" she exclaims.

I blink back tears. There goes that word again, and I laugh a little. Ecstatic to feel more alive than I've felt in a long time.

"Thank you, Eva. For everything."

Elena Used to Say

Get you a friend

That shows up for you

That sings your praises

That isn't afraid to be silly and funny and laugh

Be the kind of friend

That shows up for your friend

That sings their praises when they can't find the notes in the song

That isn't afraid to let you lean on their shoulder

That got two good shoulders and no judgment

That speaks highly of you when no one is looking

That challenges you to be better

That inspires you to do better

Monday: H.E.R. Leadership Advisory

I walk into Ms. G's room on Monday morning and return the latest borrowed book to her desk.

"What did you think?" she asks excitedly, picking up the book and holding it to the chest of her cardigan sweater. "Did you love it?"

" 'I am tired of looking at what we can't have,' " I respond, quoting a moment in *The House on Mango Street,* and a smile spreads across my entire face.

"Oh, Angel!" she almost screams, her accent bubbling up over the loudspeaker announcements as the students begin filtering into their designated homerooms.

"I really liked it. So much of it felt like my own life, it was crazy." I sigh.

"Exactly! That's how I feel about books that make me remember what home feels like. If I can see the sand; or feel the drops from my island's waterfalls; or taste my grandmother's stew chicken, ground provisions, or dumplings; or smell the steam rising from the bowl just by reading a story, I know it's exactly the out-of-body experience I've been waiting for!"

I walk over to the circle of chairs and drop my backpack next to my usual seat.

Nikki sulks into the room, silent and obviously bothered. It's the third week of October and the frost is cold and unwavering. Nikki is wearing a crop-top sweatshirt and leggings with furry UGG-style boots. She looks at me and nods. I nod.

I've come to appreciate our little talks.

Right behind her is Kamilah and Reina, both laughing, and when

they catch my attention they wave. I wave back. "How's little Avion?"
I ask as they sit down.

Reina explodes. "Oh my god—he's so smart! He turned over this
morning and almost started to cry—then he turned himself right back
over! All by himself! Kamilah caught it on video! Show her, Ma!"

Kamilah laughs as she reaches for her phone, quick to show her
pride and joy.

"Let me talk for myself, dang!" Kamilah jokes.

"That's my godbaby, I do what I want!" Reina counters, kissing
her teeth.

Teiya, her usual cup of chai in hand, smiles as she enters. "Morning,
Teiya," I offer. Whenever we see one another in the library at lunch,
we've taken to sitting next to each other on the floor, propped against
the library wall. Not talking, just sharing space. At first, I thought she
wanted to talk. But then I realized, she's a thinker, like me. And now
it's one of the bravest things anyone has ever shared with me. Space to
just be with no judgment.

Eva walks in. She's wearing a large black bubble coat and bug
glasses, similar to the ones in hip-hop legend Missy Elliott's video *The
Rain (Supa Dupa Fly)*.

"Look at Eva," Reina gushes. "She catwalk ready, yassssss!"

Everyone is laughing and talking inside the circle. Ju Ju is like a
dark cloud, and her energy enters the room before she steps foot across
the threshold. Her black-and-white Yankees fitted is low on top of a
fresh row of braids and she is wearing Ray-Ban sunglasses.

Inside the room.

She walks to sit next to Nikki's seat, and Nikki stands up so quick,
we all stop talking and watch her stomp across the circle to the empty
chair next to Teiya. Teiya sips from her cup. Nikki glares at Ju Ju. Ju Ju

keeps her glasses on but removes her baseball cap and runs her fingers through the parts of her cornrow braids in frustration. Awkward.

RaChelle is wearing a red peacoat with her blue waist-length braids in a messy bun on top of her head, when she finds her seat. She isn't wearing her glasses and her eyes dart across the room, first at Ju Ju, then past Nikki.

"Okay, H.E.R. Advisory, let's get it together! Have a seat, have a seat," Ms. G orders after putting her books back in her personal collection. She grabs her attendance sheet and notebook with her favorite fine-point pen. She clicks it alive. "I hope everyone had a great weekend." She makes eye contact with most of the class before her eyebrows furrow, finally reading the tension in the room. "I am excited to hear how you are feeling this morning." She places her notebook on her lap. Looks at Ju Ju, who is now sitting forward, forearms on her knees with her head down. "Can you start for me this morning, Angel, and can you tell us what you're excited about? I think we need some optimistic energy this Monday morning!" she adds.

This is actually my favorite part of the day. "I'm good. I'm like a nine," I start. "And I think I'm so happy because after school today I get to take this sling off."

"It's LIT!" Eva responds. And I feel like I'm glowing from the inside out.

"I'm like an eight or nine too," Eva begins. "I'm hype about the youth conference that I came back from. We made a bid to bring the quarterly convention here to Brooklyn. And I think it's going to happen. The theme is"—she takes her glasses off to punctuate each syllable dramatically—"Youth Voice for Justice." She says excitedly, "And we host over one hundred different school ambassadors for an entire day of workshops, discussion, community outreach—it's dope, y'all. I hope after our open mic this Friday, y'all can help me out with this one?" She rubs her hands together and we agree with head nods.

"That sounds really cool," Teiya says. "Today is a good day. I'm an eight. I'm excited about our open mic. I wrote a poem in Ms. G's seventh-period class and I was nervous about reading out loud, but now I think I am ready to share it." She crosses her corduroy-clad legs. Her black sweater and orange beanie make her look like she's ready to shoot an ad for stylish students who want to study abroad.

Ms. G responds, "I can't wait to hear it read out loud, Teiya. Also, hat." She motions with a warm smile.

Teiya nods and removes the beanie before placing it in her bag.

"I'm a three," Nikki says loudly. "And I'm excited to get my life back. I'm excited to not be lied to anymore. I'm excited to be with somebody who will lift me up and not put me down. Somebody who knows a good thing when they see it. Somebody who won't cheat on me!" The room is silent. But Nikki doesn't stop. "I'm excited to get my heart back from childish, lying ass—"

"Okay, okay, Nikki. Take a deep breath," Ms. G interrupts. But Nikki isn't having it. She is nearly out of her chair and on a roll.

"Nah, Ms. G! No. Ju Ju lied to me. She lied to me. She said it was me and her. Then I followed her to RaChelle's house!" Ju Ju's mouth opens. "I saw you!" Nikki almost shrieks. "You said you were out."

"I was just braiding her hair," RaChelle offers. But Nikki glares at her so hard that the whole room shudders.

"Don't even talk to me," she growls at RaChelle. "I don't care about anything you have to say. I don't have a relationship with you. I'm supposed to be with her!" She points to Ju Ju, now standing. "And you can't even take your damn glasses off. You so cool! You think it's easy for me? Coming out to my family with you? You said it was ME AND YOU!"

Nikki stands up; her feet are planted like tree trunks. Ms. G is now in front of her. Not touching her. But standing so close, Nikki moves to the left and right to make eye contact with Ju Ju. Ju Ju's glasses are now off, and I realize she is crying.

"I'm sorry, yo," she finally says. And Nikki's knees buckle. She falls back into her chair, crying. Teiya puts her hand on Nikki's shoulder and she begins to shake. She leans over and covers her eyes. "I'm sorry," Ju Ju keeps going. "I got so much love for you. You're my best friend. But . . ." And her voice trails off.

Ms. G leans in front of Nikki's chair to put a calm hand on her exposed shoulder and Reina moves over so Ms. G can take a seat.

"But what?!" Nikki wails. She lifts her head and looks at Ju Ju, pleading. "You had nothing to lose, Ju Ju."

"What?!" Ju Ju explodes. "Every single day I have something to lose!" Her voice goes hoarse and her eyes red. "I'm a gay Black girl. And just because I love who I love, I get threats just by walking down the street. I got shit to lose too, Nikki! But I can't help that RaChelle is my first love."

My mouth drops open. I never guessed they were dating, but then, I have enough rooms in this brain of mine to miss things like this. If I had a cup of tea, I would sip it.

"You said it was over!"

"IT IS OVER," RaChelle confirms. "I just braided her hair. I love Ju Ju, but not like that. Not anymore. I have a boyfriend now. We're just friends . . ."

And my mind goes foggy. For a minute, I think of Darius and the arguments we used to have. The way he would grab my shoulder or my collar. The way I threw his phone to get away. I make myself come back, deep breath in, and pull my sweatshirt to close off the cold air, like a curtain.

"You're just *what*? Friends?!" Nikki scoffs, no longer crying. She is sitting, back straight, eyes wild, and she is looking back and forth between Ju Ju and RaChelle. "You thought you were *just* friends?"

Ju Ju insists, "I did this. I tried to kiss her. But nothing happened. I was wrong. It's not her fault."

"You're right." Nikki stands up. "It is your fault." She pushes the chair back so hard it falls over with a *clank,* and stomps out of the room. Ju Ju stands up and Ms. G follows her.

"Ju Ju, stay here." Her hand is outstretched, and Ju Ju slowly sits down. Picks up her cap from the floor and leans back in her chair, eyes to the sky. Ms. G walks to the landline phone hanging on the wall.

"Mrs. B, can you assist me in my room quickly? Yes," she responds briskly. "Right now, I need to tend to a student in emotional distress."

We are all still sitting in the circle. Our eyes looking between Ju Ju, who seems to be ignoring the world, and RaChelle, who looks sick to her stomach.

"Are you okay?" Reina asks RaChelle. RaChelle shakes her head but doesn't answer immediately. When she finally opens her mouth, her voice is heavy with near tears.

"I hate to see someone so sad," she begins. "But I can't do this . . ." Her voice cracks. She's nearest to Reina, who reaches out and pats her hand awkwardly.

"It's okay," she whispers.

"Nah," Kamilah interrupts. "You knew Ju Ju still liked you, RaChelle. You ain't supposed to have her over at your house braiding hair or nothing. You know how she feels about you. Why would you play with her like that? If you ain't trynna be with her, you should just stay away from her." Kamilah goes back to looking at her cell phone.

"That's not fair," Eva interjects. "She didn't do anything wrong.

Why should she be blamed for being nice? Besides, what this room needs right now is—"

"Spare me the Kumbaya bull, Sistah Eva!" Kamilah replies smartly. "Y'all know what it is. Stop acting like they weren't just dating last school year! The fact they in this class after all that mess went down is a miracle."

"Why can't we be friends?" RaChelle challenges. Her eyes are rock hard. She crosses her arms before nodding at Kamilah. "We can't be friends 'cause you and your baby daddy can't be friends?"

"Bitch." Kamilah jumps up. Reina is in front of her in seconds. "Talk about my child's father again!"

"You went too far, RaChelle. Shut up," Reina warns.

"I'm not scared of you, Kamilah. They may be, but I'm not. I said it once and I'll say it again. I love my boyfriend. I *choose* my boyfriend. But that doesn't mean I need to be angry at Ju Ju every time I see her."

"You're so thirsty!" Kamilah stamps her feet like a step-team captain. "And I don't care about none of this—really. Y'all whole thing"— her hands are swirling in the air—"takes up so much space! You know she likes you, RaChelle! And you just keep playing games. Don't worry about me—you need to be afraid of yourself! Look at what you did to their relationship. All because you want your cake with icing and candles and shit!"

"Hey!" Mrs. B booms, standing at the door of the classroom; Ms. G is already gone. We didn't even notice her arrival. "Language, ladies. Seriously, Kamilah, you are someone's mother. And, RaChelle, just last semester you were fighting over Ju Ju. So, everyone, please. Take a deep breath and have a seat." Her voice is so deep I barely recognize it. And the woman who is usually sweet as syrup stands with her arms crossed. Her eyes the color of burnt hazelnuts.

Déjà Vu

In the past, when Amir and I were arguing over the remote or the last bowl of cereal or whatever, Elena would growl, "I don't want to hear it!" And we would talk under our breath (but not too loud) about what was fair and who was her favorite. This moment definitely felt like that.

RaChelle opens her mouth and Mrs. B says it matter-of-factly: "I. Don't. Want. To. Hear. It. You are juniors and seniors! You are preparing for the last year and the next stage of your life. Some of you are already well into the next step of your life." She looks to Kamilah, who is back sitting in her seat but fuming. "This behavior will not fly, ladies. This program is special, do you understand that?" She sits in Ms. G's vacated seat. "I chose each of you. I chose each of you to work with Ms. G. She is amazing, heavily sought after, and could have worked with anyone, but I chose you! Each of you has shown in your grades the quality of leadership; however, your lack of discipline is unacceptable.

"The world is waiting to eat you alive!" she continues. "The world is waiting for you to fight each other and tear each other down. The world cares more about you on television and Twitter, swinging and berating each other, than they do when you lift each other up!" Mrs. B crosses her bangle-heavy arms. "This specific Advisory is about sister-hood and unity."

Kamilah rolls her eyes and Mrs. B holds her hand up in peace. "I agree, some of you have shown more progress than others—but all of you are the leaders this school needs. This *world* needs. A year from now, you will be deciding which college you want to attend. Or which country you want to visit. So, I need you to speak to each other like the brilliant young minds you are."

Some of us nod in agreement. Even Ju Ju, RaChelle, and Kamilah seem to agree, but they don't show it.

"Don't make me regret my decision," she says firmly.

I Know Love Like

calling each other in the middle of the night

Just to hear one another breathing as you fall asleep

I know love can take its toll

It can take you away from your family

It can take your eye off the horizon

Where there is love

There is hope

And that's where I thought I could live

Forever

The thing about love is there are no rules

There is no knob to turn on or off

There is no order

There is no blueprint

Sometimes it's working fine

And then the next day

It can be gone

A vinyl record skipping on its own

A light bulb blown out

After school is over, I can't get out of the building fast enough. There are so many things I want to do and not enough time in the day. I want to head to my usual seat in the park, sit under the sun until it traces the sky into a new color of dizzy. I want to listen to the new JiggyStax playlist. I was scrolling the page during my usual lunch period in the library. Teiya to my left, both of our backs against the wall, when I saw a new track uploaded: *Angel Eyes.* I want to finish mixing my very first playlist.

Lately, the moment I finish a good book—the kind of book that makes me feel everything—I want to hear the music in the world. Instead of going quiet, like normal. I take my laptop to the fire escape and sit by the railing on a throw pillow. It's cold, even with my puff coat from the thrift store. But the air is crisp and the shuttle train traveling north up Franklin Avenue to Prospect Park keeps me company. Every twenty minutes, the wheels rumble, vibrate, and screech, a steel signal of *you are here.*

My first playlist was an accident. I was checking out all my favorite songs saved from all the artists, producers, and DJs I follow on Sound-Cloud. Different DJ sets from my favorites, like DJ Reborn, DJ JiggyStax, RL Grime, DJ Noize, and DJ Va$htie, keep me moving, but sometimes I felt like I needed something different. I can't put my finger on it. Like the groove would be there and then it was just bass, or it was just rap, or it was an electronic sound spilling out my speakers. When I went to play back my favorites, something different happened. Before, the DJs dictated my mood, and my feelings, even the sound of my heartbeat. But when I played back my favorites, something happened to the air.

Now, when Uncle Spence was running with his neighborhood

track crew, RunTellDat, at the park nearby, I found a seat near the window. Turned my Bluetooth speakers up and built a groove. TBH, Uncle tried to get me to join his neighborhood running meetup bright and early on Saturday mornings, but the crack-of-dawn hours, my sleepy face, and my arm brace made for a great excuse to stay home and fall into a musical rabbit hole. My sling was off more these days, so I knew the sensation in my fingers when I timed the perfect song combinations wasn't the usual sleepy-arm syndrome. No, this was different.

Everything felt like it was moving fast: wave patterns in the air, sound in my hair, my blood racing to the beat, my mind thinking of a thousand different things: orchids and cherry blossoms, subways and redwood trees. I was transported to every place I'd ever read or seen or dreamed about in fast-forward motion, like a movie. My head swam in the beat and a twitch in my fingers sprang the forward button to the next title.

When the next beat dropped—sure, it wasn't mixed or even perfect in its transition—it was a powerful feeling. I realized: *I decide the vibe.* I could make people feel the way I felt when reading a good book or listening to a dope DJ. It was the beginning of something beautiful. And I want to make beautiful things. But first, I want to go to Dr. Patterson's and get rid of this sling.

Waiting for the B46 to get to the hospital in East New York, I almost forget the tension of the day. But a baby crying in the stroller next to me reminds me of Kamilah and little Avion. After RaChelle and Reina had a stare-down, Kamilah looked to Reina and said, "I can't be here. I want to hurt that girl." She took a deep breath. "But I can't let down my son." The school has a zero-tolerance policy, which means you fight, whether you started it or not—no exceptions—you were out.

Kamilah had a reputation for being one of the kids that just happened to get away with fighting because she never got caught in the act. And for a while, Kamilah liked this myth. But when she had

Avion, everything changed. One day at the park, while Reina and her godson played on a swing set, she said, "That little boy saved my life. I was on the wrong path, Angel. I was headed nowhere fast. Because my anger. Because my boyfriend. Because my neighborhood. Shoot, my brother couldn't stop me from running the streets and fighting. It got so bad, I wanted to fight him! But then Avion made it all make sense. My life had to mean something more than this or I was going to end up just like my mother."

Kamilah and Sterling were both adopted by their aunt, Patty, a social worker in the food stamp office located in the shadows of downtown Brooklyn.

Kamilah's mother was in jail since Sterling was five, she revealed one day after an intense advisory session. "I was six years old when I saw her bash a woman's head with a glass bottle. The woman was cheating with my father, I think." Kamilah wiped the grass from her hands.

"I don't know. The woman lived, but my mother was charged with assault and battery. When CPS came to take us, my aunt, Patty, yoked us both up and never looked back. My mother signed over her rights, but you can't unsee things like that, ya know?"

And I nodded without a second passing. I knew exactly what she meant.

I knew what it was like for people to decide your family for you. I knew what it was like for people to try and puppet-master your life. That was what took me away from my brother and sisters. Kamilah shook her head and mumbled, "It's probably why I'm so jacked up now."

"You're not jacked up. You just built up so many defenses to protect yourself, and now Avion. It takes time to put down your guard," I offered. Twirling the grass between my fingers.

"You sound like Mrs. B," she chuckled.

A Little Bit About Mrs. B

Mrs. B says, "You control your now. You control your reaction. Every foot forward is of your choosing, so choose well." I heard Ju Ju call her Yoda once and I giggled, but then I realized that would make me a Jedi. I have taken to Mrs. B more than I expected. When I work in the office and have finished all that was set aside for me, Mrs. B doesn't mind when I listen to my playlist or finish the latest book selection. And when that gets old, I listen to the stories around me.

Mrs. B was transferred into Banneker High to help hire new teachers with a solid plan to do three things:

1) Enrich the student population often disregarded because of their economic status. *That means: give the kids in the hood the same thing they give kids in the 'burbs.*

2) Alleviate the aggression that plagued the campus. *That means: zero tolerance. No fighting. No drugs. No gangbangers.*

3) Create an environment of culture leaders who receive opportunities for higher learning rather than being kicked out of the school because of a few mistakes. *That means: see us as future leaders, not criminals.*

Word has it, Mrs. B once helped run the superintendent's office for District 13 and had the best results. Her graduation rates skyrocketed, her testing scores matched private schools' in Manhattan's privileged areas, and her students went on to work in policy making after receiving full-ride scholarships to CUNY and SUNY. Mrs. B has a pride to her. And she requires young people to walk and treat one another with pride too. She doesn't allow security guards to speak down to students, and she insists students behave like the best version of their young adult selves.

Eva tells me, "Mrs. B isn't just some principal's secretary. She is the mother-in-law of Principal Stern. She was once a principal herself."

Want to Hear a Love Story?

Over thirty years ago, Mrs. B fell in love with her husband, the principal of a neighboring school outside of her district, and it was love at first sight. Word has it, he mispronounced her name: Mariame Adichie. He apologized profusely, with roses and courting. She kissed her teeth at the attempt to win over her heart. They married three months later. Started their family within a year while she ran an Afrocentric children's day-care educational center in Bedford-Stuyvesant, Brooklyn. She began it to ensure their two children, a girl and a boy, would receive the cultural enrichment and educational excellence she found lacking in the current school system. And after fifteen years of teaching neighborhood children their alphabets, compassion through song, mathematics, science, cooking, and urban gardening, while celebrating their roots throughout the African diaspora, Mrs. B implemented language classes to the graduating grade, so by the time her students entered first grade they all spoke Spanish, Swahili, and English.

When her husband became superintendent of District 13, he asked her to become a principal and help turn the tide of an academic high school on the verge of being shut down. Her two children, now in high school, had long complained about the kinds of teachers they endured. And as they prepared to go to college—her daughter was settling into the oldest college in New York, an Ivy League institution bordering Harlem, and her son prepared to go to school in the small town of Binghamton, in upstate New York—she sold her day-care center and accepted the superintendent's challenge. She implemented the same core values into the high school, and within five years it became one of the leading high schools in the city. In ten years, it became one of the top-performing high schools in the state. Mrs. B was an inspiration.

I Ain't Never Seen Anyone

Like Mrs. B

She's kind

The kind of Black woman

Who tells the truth

But wipes your nose when you cry

Broken heart?

Missing your parent?

She got the remedy

Mrs. B has the most visitors

Past students who walk taller

Because she says your name

Because she's not the same as other adults

Yeah, she's stern

She's quick to the point

But no one has to guess where she stands

She stands with the students

She says we are today's leaders on the verge of becoming

She says it with so much passion

You begin to believe her

Open Mic

The open mic has transformed the library into a real life–looking-ass café! There are fake candles on these small stools with assorted flowers and cups of chai or hot chocolate at a nearby library table turned bar. White cheddar popcorn and granola bars line the top with a hand-made calligraphy-style sign that reads: *Take One!*

A microphone stand with a bunch of scarves tied to the top is centered in front of the memoir section. Sure, the stage is just an old carpet, but under the skylight it looks just like a spotlight. Ju Ju is the DJ and she's taking her job seriously. She sings along to all the hits she drops. Songs by Lil Baby, Drake, Ari Lennox, and Princess Nokia weave in and out of the speakers through the room. She laughs and points to the crowd, which makes it easy for folks to want to sing along too. We all pile into this renewed space, beaming.

Sterling walks in and we catch eyes quick. I give him a small wave and his eyes light up when he nods. Teiya sits next to me on the floor. She crosses her legs and hands me a cup of chai. The library has become a sanctuary for me. I'm used to hiding here with Teiya during the day. It gives me a chance to take a deep breath. And just be. It was also where I wrote my first poem.

The sign-up list is being passed around. Ms. G sits by the door and sways to the beat. But when Vybz Kartel comes on she stands up to whine a little. The dance is like the washing machine, something Elena used to tell me was her favorite dance growing up. I laugh unexpectedly.

"What's so funny?" Teiya asks, bringing me out of my spell.

"Nothing." I sigh. "I'm just happy," I admit. Teiya gives me an interesting look, like she wants to ask more questions, but the show is beginning. Eva takes to the stage as the host of the open mic.

"If you can hear me, say 'YEAH'!" she orders. And the whole room erupts. The energy is kinetic. It moves everything in the space. Even the books seem to lean toward Eva's instructions. "If you ready to start this open mic, say 'OH YEAH'!" she adds. And the skylight shakes in agreement.

"Bet. This is how we're going to do it. Imma call your name and say 'on deck' to let you know to get ready to share your work. Then Imma call up the poet who's gonna share their work right now. Poems can be whatever you want them to be. Ask me how I know." She smiles and takes a beat.

"How do you know?" the audience responds. Folks already know their job at the open mic and I giggle. This is wild!

Eva goes, "Poetry can do it all. It can be a song, a rap, a poetic short story, or a monologue! Ask me how I know." She smiles and this time I jump in with the rest.

"How do you know?"

"Because Edgar Allan Poe said 'Poetry is the rhythmical creation of beauty in words,' but really—everything you do is poetry. And we're going to celebrate everyone who touches this stage. We clap for courage when each poet gets on stage and we snap for success. Are you with me? Say 'word'!"

"Word," we all yell.

"Ight, Banneker! On deck is Amari, but the first poet on the mic is Angel!"

The crowd erupts with thunderous applause.

New Ways to See Myself

When no one is looking

I see who I could be

I could be the girl that swings at the sky

or

I could be the girl who never gets it right

The music only knows my fears

Each song I play is what my blood needs near

To resist the fear of being

    No more fights

    No more tears

    No more silence

    No more loneliness

This world has enough room for my wingspan

And if it doesn't

I'll split the sky in half

Swing my sound until the ceiling shatters

I'm still here

And I'm still worthy of love

The day I'm headed to my last hospital visit with a sling, I wave good-bye to Mrs. B. She waves and calls out, "Congrats, sweetheart! Chin up!" before turning her attention back to her computer. A student wanders into the room and I almost skip out. I'm so excited. On my way to living sling-less.

I push the red button on the bright yellow pole of the B26 bus and wait for the next stop. I am eager to head through the double doors of the hospital, where Uncle Spence is already waiting for me at the front desk. He's wearing dark blue scrubs and is laughing with a security guard next to a sign that reads INFORMATION. I wave and smile and head toward him.

"There's my niece!" He greets me. "This is Bao." He introduces me to the guard. "He's been working here since I first arrived. . . ."

"Long before yuh an dey neva let mi guh." He is an older man with hands the size of small hammers, but his eyes shine. His accent makes me smile. And I laugh as Uncle says goodbye, walking us up the first flight of stairs to another set of doors and crossing an enclosed glass bridge. When I first arrived in Brooklyn, I got lost every single time. But now I know the maze in my sleep.

"How was school?" Uncle asks, pushing the bright blue wheelchair button and waiting for a nurse and an older woman in a wheelchair to move past us.

"Thank you." They smile and pass.

"Today was crazy, Unc." I start remembering Advisory class. "But I'm excited to be here and see Dr. P. How is she?"

"There you go." He shakes his head. We are waiting at the elevator bank.

"What?" I smile innocently. Dr. P and Uncle would make such a cute couple. And I know my uncle dated someone before I moved here. But I haven't met anyone since I stepped foot into the house. I asked once after our breakfast of champions (bacon, egg, and cheese on a roll), "Why is that?"

And he replied, "I'm too busy building my Kingdom. When I meet her, I want to be ready." Uncle doesn't go into it too deep. He also doesn't tell me who "her" is or what "ready" looks like.

When we exit the elevator onto the fourth floor, we enter room 413 down the hall and I sign the visitors' log. Uncle remains at the nurses' reception desk and talks to Yvette. She's always nice when she sees me. It's funny. I used to hear so many stories about New York City being mean, but it's been one of the nicest places I've been. Sure, I lived in California for most of my life—but I visited a lot of cities: Stockton, Fresno, Reno, Bakersfield, Oakland, and Pomona.

"Hey, T!" a voice full of laughter calls from the door. And I swing my head back to the door to see Dr. Patterson walk in wearing her usual outfit: white coat, washed-out blue scrubs, and a pair of white Nike Huaraches. She is carrying two cups of coffee and hands one to Yvette.

"Here you go, Vette," she says before standing next to Uncle Spence and smirking. "And you like white mocha, right?" Uncle's face gets warm. I can tell, because his freckles almost disappear, and I know for a fact UNCLE SPENCE LIKES DR. P!

"Wow, you remembered," he laughs.

"Yep," she says, and hands him a cup of coffee.

"Aw, man, you're too good to me. I feel special," he adds, taking the cup, and I swear I think I see their hands touch.

I want a closer look. But Dr. P is already moving to the door that leads to the examination rooms, says over her shoulder, "You better."

"I got you next time," he calls after her. "I'll wait out here for you, Angel." I move past him to the door and nod, but his eyes are fastened to Dr. P's.

"Come on, Angel Love," she calls to me. I never thought I'd like the nickname, but I feel special when she says it. Dr. P is looking directly into Uncle's eyes and adds, "I hope so."

And now I know for a super fact: DR. P LIKES UNCLE SPENCE TOO! I slip into Exam Room A and hop on the table, smiling from ear to ear. Dr. P lifts the ugly, worn-out, stretched-out, food-and-makeup-stained right-arm prison from my shoulder for the last time, and it's like I hear a full orchestra begin to play "Right Hand Man." (You know, the song from the *Hamilton* musical when they introduce George Washington?)

In my head I hear a five-piece string section, percussions, and a set of drums. She tosses aside the Velcro madness and I wiggle my fingers freely, stretch my elbow north then south to her approval. When she gives a nod and turns her back to me to look at my medical file, I hear the cast from *Hamilton* as they take center stage: "Here comes the general! Rise up!"

Rise Up

Before Thanksgiving break, we are assigned the task of fact-checking the accuracy of *Hamilton: An American Musical* using Howard Zinn's *A People's History of the United States* and should return before winter break ready to debate, battle rap style. Split into groups of four, and Eva is in my group and naturally she takes the lead. She has a Google group set up and document open when we are placed in a group with two other juniors: Malcolm, who wears a Dominican flag embroidered on the sleeve of his jean jacket, and Miles, a Trinidadian with long dreadlocks swinging past the middle of his back. He wears all-black everything all the time; the only splash of color is his tortoise-shell glasses.

Malcolm is a great rapper, he's a basketball player, and he walks around in Gucci sneakers. He always talks about my eyes being pretty, licks his lips like a music video, and asks me what Cali is like. He's a Harlem kid, moved to Brooklyn to live with his grandmother, who used to go to church with Mrs. B. I'm not interested in him at all. I'm trying to focus on my next move in life, so I friendzone his Pretty Ricky act real quick and he doesn't even blink. There are so many girls dropping their pens near him, trying to get his attention, and he's too busy taking selfies with them in the school hallways to care.

His best friend, Miles, isn't a ballplayer but the school president, and he's head over heels for Eva. They argue all the time about everything from insights on Instagram to social platforms as tools for the CIA to track American citizens. Sometimes I don't even know what they're talking about. It feels like I've been given a different textbook all this time. But I'm not defeated, just hungrier to learn. This is when Malcolm and I huddle up and exchange bars.

M: *Color lines rely*
On the power of the dollar

A: *Racism doesn't happen in reverse*
It's the American curse

M: *They use slavery as free labor*
Black children born into hell

A: *Ain't much changed today*
Because prisons operate the same

Before moving to Brooklyn, I would never have guessed that I would be a good MC, but my lyrics are fresh! I think I'm becoming good at writing the raps, and Malcolm is a natural at performing, so we have a perfect formula for acing the assignment. When Eva and Miles are done arguing, they return to the fold and give their opinions on which parts of the truth need to be highlighted in our rhymes. It feels like a perfect combination.

Back to Life, Back to Reality

My arm moves like it once did, before the accident. Dr. P instructs me to move the arm counterclockwise then clockwise. She scribbles notes and asks if I have any pain.

"I don't have any pain," I lie. I have a little pain. It's tight beneath my shoulder blade. But I don't want to wear that Velcro trap anymore!

Dr. P raises an eyebrow. "It's okay if it's a little tight. That will go away with time and exercise." It's like she can read my mind. "But if you don't tell me the whole truth, Angel, I can't help you."

She looks me square in the eyes.

"Okay. It hurts a little bit," I admit. "Just a little. But I'm ready to be out of that thing, Dr. P! I can't take it anymore."

She sighs deep. "Look. You still need to go to physical therapy once a week, okay? And here, take this rubber ball." She places a fist-sized blue handball into my palm. "Squeeze," she orders, and I do with a wince. It's tight and my shoulder blade feels like sharp pins are everywhere.

I keep my face still, keep my eyes cold.

"Squeeze and release twenty times, count to four, then release. Repeat this three times a day. No heavy lifting. No push-ups or pull-ups. And no fighting." She looks away quickly.

I squeeze the ball to feel the sharp pins. I squeeze the ball to forget how it got this bad in the first place.

Rewind: Black, Black, Black, Black on Black

When I wake up on a gurney, I look around and the sky is dark blue. Ambulance lights dance against the shadows of the trees and street-lights. Darius is seated in the back of a patrol car. I try to say his name. But my mouth is so dry. I try to sit up, but I'm strapped down. I grimace and try to look to my right when I realize I can't really see. Everything goes: black, black, black, black. Somehow, now I'm above my gurney, I think. My vision is blurry, but I think I see the gurney. Someone is lying on the gurney, but I can't see who. Then a set of hands covers the body with a white sheet and rolls away briskly. A scream escapes my lips before everything goes black again.

Black, black, black, black on black

Black, my thoughts so black

Black, black, I'm black

My skin is so black, I'm rockin' that black on black, it's black

Black rims on these black wheels, in this black whip.

I decide to walk home from my meeting with Dr. Patterson. Uncle Spence sees me to the front door, and I say farewell to Mr. Bao, still seated and reading the newspaper, unbothered at the front desk.

"I'll be home a little late," Uncle warns me. "Text me when you get home."

The route will take about thirty minutes and if I move quick enough, I can miss the dinner rush at Ali's Roti Shop. Ali's is a Trinidad food staple in Brooklyn. When I first tried the roti, I couldn't understand how it was so sweet and savory, the chicken, chickpeas, and tamarind wrapped inside the best kind of layered dough. The yummy full feeling after a fresh-prepared roti is similar to the delicious euphoria I remember whenever Amir and I pooled our money to share a carne asada burrito platter from the back of Jimmie's taco van near our house.

Ali's line is intricate. Folks waiting for their chance to place their order with the no-nonsense auntie preparing plates from smoking tin pots full of stewed meats and vegetables understood the rules: anybody that entered the glass storefront knew better than to *block her blasted door and dare not leave it open to disrupt her concentration and bring in the cold.*

Customers fall in a neat circle as tight as a millipede's body in retreat. The smell when the bell rings as I open the door is much lovelier than I remember. Seven minutes later, when I take my first bite into the pumpkin-and-callaloo-filled roti with sautéed strips of chicken, onions, and love, I am so happy and delirious I forget rush hour is near and folks bundled up in their puff jackets and scarves are hurrying to their warm homes. I bump into someone, mouth full and eyes nearly closed, but manage to throw my right hand up in apology. "Sorry," I mumble, covering my mouth.

"Angel?" Sterling replies. He's holding my shoulder to steady me. And I'm holding on to my roti for dear life.

I finish chewing and gulp. "Sterling! What are you doing over here?"

"I live a couple of blocks away." He smiles. "Look at you! Your sling is gone!" His whole face is a light. A beautiful brown light.

I swallow a gulp of air this time. Reach in the plastic bag and search for my small soda bottle of Pink Ting.

"How have you been?" I ask, my heart racing, but I am calm. Too calm. This is weird.

"I'm good," he responds easily. We move out of the walkway and I wrap my roti in its wax paper and foil and tuck it safely into my plastic bag. "You rock with Ali's, huh?" He laughs.

"Yeah, it's hella good!" I respond quickly. My Cali ways slipping out of my mouth effortlessly.

"Hella, huh?" He laughs, a full belly laugh. It's the first time I've seen him this happy without Avion in his arms. "I almost forgot you were from California." He straightens up, smooths out his black North Face and gray knitted cap over his ears. "It's getting cold out. Where you headed?"

"I'm headed home," I say. Tuck the precious bag of food in my backpack and carry my open bottle of Ting. I point with the bottle and start moving.

"I'll walk you a bit, cool?"

I nod and sip from the emptying bottle. "Where's Avion?" I ask.

"He's probably home with Kamilah. I was scheduled to work, but they told me they overstaffed folks, so I decided to come home early and hang out with them. You ever been to the West Indian Day Parade?" he asks as we cross the parkway.

I read about it before, but I never got to experience it.

"On Labor Day weekend, it's wild, yo! This whole parkway stretches for miles as millions of people wine, dance, and chip behind their float." I shake my head in amazement. "Truly! The whole way. DJ and tunes and costumes—it's live, man." And for the first time I hear a bit of Sterling's island accent. It's nice, the way he can carry the words like their own song.

"That's dope."

"Yeah, we all we got, ya know? And we get to celebrate our culture."

Rewind: Carnival Is Like

At one of our biweekly brunches, Uncle Spence explained Carnival to me.

Uncle: The West Indian culture and the Carnival tradition is a three-day nonstop fête full of feathers and bodysuits, glitter and sneakers. The steel pans and rum punch swim in the air and spill on the entire blacktop of the parkway.

Me: The entire parkway?

Uncle: On every side, it stretches and the people spill everywhere. It's hard to explain, you have to see it for yourself.

Me: Come on, Unc. What is it like?

Uncle: I can't do it justice with my words. You see it for yourself.

Me: But if you could put it into words, what would you say?

Uncle: I'd say the streets are filled with Mack trucks that transform into floats. The beds of these trucks are lined with people-sized speakers made of wood and electronic heartbeats. The street is filled with dancers and DJs, turntables, and costumes the size of cars! I'd say the streets are filled with women from every place on the map, vibrant makeup streaking their faces in lime greens and fuchsia pink. Silver stripes and Black black matte lipsticks. The streets are alive with men wearing glitter and white chalk, or black oil and red paint placed strategically on their faces. Paint is tossed in the air and damp bodies dance and jump to the riddim, their hands up and bodies gyrating as their voices and air horns pierce the sky.

Me: You sound like a poet, Unc!

Uncle: Rappers are poets too! Like I said, every year the parade ends with thousands of people rushing the blue police barricades to dance to the reggae, soca, and calypso sounds as if their lives depend on it. Flags from every Caribbean island are represented on the parkway.

Me: Jamaica? Trinidad?

Uncle: Yes and yes. Of course.

Me: St. Croix? Haiti?

Uncle: Yep and most definitely! They won Band of the Year a couple of times.

Me: Dominica? Guadeloupe?

Uncle: Can I finish? Like I said, *everybody.* And the vendors? My mouth waters just thinking about the pepper shrimp, the smell of fried fish and plantains, the sweet peanut punch, and baked macaroni pie. And there are grocery baskets full of flags, chilled water bottles, and nutcrackers made of mango, lemons, or soursop. And big—I mean, *huge*—plastic jugs of sea moss line the service roads with the best seats in the house.

Me: I can't wait to see this.

Uncle: Me too, niece. The joy, the music, the vast cultures that are different and still very similar, is in the air and it touches everything.

But, Today

The gray stretch of road of the parkway is filled with private yellow school buses with black Hebrew letters and white-and-blue MTA buses filled to the brim. Uber and Lyft drivers head toward the airport, or the city. Today, the service road islands are occupied by wobbly card tables full of tube socks and incense sticks, fragrance, knit gloves (two for five dollars), skullcaps and scarves with "We Run Brooklyn" in bold white letters.

Today, I do not marvel at all the beauty of Brooklyn. I am distracted by Sterling's smile.

Him: What's the last movie you watched?
Me: Something on Netflix. It was about the ballroom dance scene in NYC and Christopher Street. My turn.

Me: What's your favorite thing to do in Brooklyn?
Him: Walk the Brooklyn Bridge while eating froyo from Pinkberry. Don't look at me like that; froyo is Gucci.

Him: Do you miss California? What was it like?
Me: I miss the weather sometimes. How the sun is always out and beating hot, even when there is a little bit of wind. And I miss my little brother all the time. His name is Amir. I miss him the most. I miss the cars pulling up in an empty parking lot and folks opening their doors and turning up their sound systems. Music for days just pouring out: old-school NWA, new hyphy sounds, Funkadelic tracks with Bootsie Collins and Tupac. Really, I miss the sound of Cali, when the crickets and grasshoppers made their own music.

Me: What are you going to do when you graduate?
Him: My aunt wants me to go to Howard University to study engineering. She thinks I can save neighborhoods like ours if I understand how to talk the language with contractors and businesses that buy property and push out the poor people.
Me: What do you want to do?

Him: I mean, I want to go to college too. But I love music. And I want to see the world.

Him: What's the weirdest compliment you ever heard?
Me: I don't really remember the nice things people say.
Him: Why not?
Me: Because they aren't real. How people treat you—that's the test.
Him: How do people treat you?
Me: I don't know. Like crap?
Him: I can't see that. Even when you try to act tough, I can tell you're nice.
Me: People get treated like crap every day. I'm no different.
Him: I think you're different.

Me: What is it like growing up in Brooklyn?
Him: It's like running after Mr. Softee and never catching him. It's like free entry to the Botanical Garden. It's like block parties with a DJ set up and water balloon fights. It's like wining and lime with your family and friends. It's like everyone sitting on the stoop and nobody fighting. It's like a house party in the middle of Fort Greene Park, and free music concerts during the Celebrate Brooklyn Festival. It's like school shopping at VIM if you're lucky. It's everybody rushing home from school to sit on the stoop and joke and share chicken wings with mambo sauce. It's like Chinese food takeout and sweet iced tea. It's like the first snowflake. It's like the worst snowstorm when even the ambulance couldn't get down the street to help people in need. It's like winter freezing the pipes and boiling hot water for a bath. It's like parties everywhere because we can.

We are standing in front of the Franklin shuttle. Four blocks from my house and two blocks from the bougie pizza shop. "Have you eaten there?" he asks.

I shake my head. "My uncle Spence doesn't believe in their pizza," I start. "He says, 'Our family only eats Not Ray's!'" And we both topple over in laughter.

"Yo! Deadass, your uncle is right. Not Ray's slaps!"

"Thanks for walking me, Sterling," I say reluctantly. The sun is almost down now and the cold is biting at the skin beneath my extra pair of leggings. "I should probably get home. And you too! You're pretty far away," I add.

"Nah, Imma just jump on the train. I'll be home in no time."

"See you tomorrow," I begin. "Tell Kamilah I said hi."

"Cool," he says, and turns to the subway slowly. "Yo, Angel," he calls back. "If I give you my number will you text me?"

Playlist Title: I'm Feeling Myself

After walking with Sterling last week, I go missing. I fall into school-work and anything that will keep my mind off Sterling. I finish my part of the history project and email the lyrics to our group thread. I sign up for the yoga meditation class that begins in January. I finish Ms. G's books over the weekend and spend Sunday falling into the rabbit hole that is YouTube.

On a random Thursday, Uncle is called in for a double shift. I decide to check out the library before the sun sets, and in the midst of looking for the new Jason Reynolds book, I discover a youth poetry slam happening in the basement of the Brooklyn Library. Climbing down the fire exit stairs, I almost feel like I'm walking into a bat cave. But when the basement door opens, it's a beautiful theater with two sets of double doors and thick carpet paving the way.

Young people fill the auditorium and there is a line on the side of the stage to sign up to share original poems. A dozen youth poets climb the stairs and share their hearts. One boy walks onstage, he's wearing a gray hoodie and headphones are around his neck. He pulls his hood off and I realize it's Biz. I slouch down further in my chair toward the back of the auditorium. He snaps his brown fingers in front of the mic to test the volume, then begins.

Biz Goes

Watch the hand

They don't want us to win

Watch the man

Always a bird in the hand

And several birds in the bushes

The government's branches are on fire

Fire?!

You ain't seen nothing

Till you witnessed my mama burning

Fish on the stove with onions and hot grease

She makes a meal out of nothing

She makes a man out of me and my brothers

My mother is the earth

And this country stay trynna torch her

Dear Lord,

I watch my mama lean into a prayer

In your name

Church every Sunday

Bible study on Tuesday

Watch the hand

Watch us grow

They don't want us to win

That much we know

It's like all the lights go bright. Big bright. The crowd is clapping and some fellas standing in the aisle hoot and holler in approval. I am moved. I usually only hear him say "Angel Eyes" or "Shorty"—I am clapping because I feel so close to his story. Thinking about Elena and how she worked to make sure we had food to eat. Thinking about Biz's poem, I almost cry. After the poetry slam is over, I see Biz on the way out. He walks over. "Good job, Biz. I liked your poem."

Biz's eyes light up. "Word? You like that, huh?"

Instantly I regret the compliment. And Biz sees me shut down.

"I'm playing, I'm playing. Thank you, Angel. What you doing here?"

I shrug.

"Well, I'm glad you made it. You should come next month. I try something new every time."

"That's what's up," I offer. "See you," I call over my shoulder as I head out.

"Yo, wait up," Biz calls. "Let me walk you."

"I'm okay, I don't live too far," I say, moving toward the stairs.

"Damn, let me be a gentleman." Biz sighs. "Is that okay? Can I walk you, Miss Mean?"

I laugh. "Me, mean?"

Biz straightens his hoodie. "Yeah. I been trying to holler at you and you keep acting like you don't hear me."

I roll my eyes. "That's not it. I just got a lot going on."

"I just want to be friends, Ma."

"See, that's the thing, my name ain't Ma. And how you want to be friends but you call me everything but my name?"

Biz's shoulders fall a little. "You right. Let me try again, okay?"

"For real?"

"Deadass."

I laugh. "Okay, fine. You can walk me up the block. But this is just a friendly walk, right?"

He smiles bright and it's the first time I realize he has dimples.

"Word!" He points at a group of friends still standing in the aisle by the stage. "Yo! I hit you later, Ek, Tah, Terence!" And we set out. The dark-blue sky creeping toward nightfall. The mahogany doors close with a thump.

I Decide Biz Ain't So Bad

The walk home isn't as bad as I thought. I find out we like the same music. And both are obsessed with *In Living Color* and *Living Single*.

He go: Yo, Khadijah is my girl!

I go: Everybody your girl, you said that about Lisa Bonet too!

He go: Lisa Bonet is fine! Have you seen her daughter?

I go: Zoë Kravitz?

He go: Word!

I go: You're right—she is fine!

He go: Yo, you wild, Angel!

I go: Yeah, I know.

He go: You from California, right?

I go: Yeah, where you from?

He go: Trinidad, home of the hottest calypso, soca, and peppers!

I go: Oh, okay.

He go: I eat one pepper on the side of my plate every day. Every meal.

I go: That's wild! Ghost pepper and Scotch bonnets?

He go: Alladat! I'm a Carnival Baby so, you know, the hotter the better!

I go: Oh, boy. There you go.

He go: You know you want to laugh. Come on, come with me.

And we laugh like old friends. Like easy friends. The walk ain't as bad as I thought. But it ain't like walking with Sterling either. Biz and I walk around Grand Army Plaza and find a bench hidden from blaring car horns zooming through the roundabout. We sit and talk about our moms for a while. Really, he talks and I listen. His mom is a home nurse for a woman in their building. His little brothers are both soccer players in middle school. They are twins. We got the identical super siblings thang in common. His moms left when his father was mowed down in Trinidad, and I think, *Wow. We got that in common too.* When Biz isn't putting on a show for everybody else, he's pretty cool.

He wipes the dirt off the toe of his Air Force 1s and looks at me. "What about your moms?"

I've been feeling the cold needle of homesickness lately. I think if I talk about Elena, I might start to cry.

"She sent me here. That's it." I shrug and decide listening to him talk about his mom is home enough. For now.

Tending Wounds

I find more things to busy myself with. I finish my proposal for Mr. Jackson's botany winter assignment. I buy two newly budding potted plants from a Black-owned garden called Natty's.

I put one plant on my windowsill, directly in the sunlight. And I put the other potted plant on the floor of the closet. The one in the closet has earbuds and my first playlist playing one hour a day. The plant on the windowsill has no music. My hypothesis is, *Do plants grow more in the dark surrounded by sound or do they grow more in the light but lonely?* I take pictures and scribble notes of their progress every day. By the time we return in January I will have the results.

The second week after my walk with Sterling, instead of calling him, I tell myself how busy I need to be. I can't fall into a relationship with nobody. I'm still tending to my wounds.

The second week, I don't see him in the hallway. I don't know if I'm hiding from him, or he's hiding from me.

When I see Biz in school during period change it's pretty chill. We wave, and sometimes if he's posted at the security desk, he'll walk me to Mrs. B's office. He's been different ever since the poetry slam at the Brooklyn Library. Which is good, because I think we could be friends.

I finally begin my physical therapy sessions. My first time in PT, Dr. Patterson joins me to make sure I'm not alone. Uncle Spence asked her to check on me while he's on shift at the hospital.

I didn't know how much it meant until I see her standing at the door and something claws up my throat, itching and raw. I cough until tears are coming out of my eyes. She smiles when she sees me. She's not wearing her usual white coat, but a pair of fitted jeans and black heeled motorcycle boots. Her hair in a messy bun and her bangs swing across her forehead.

"Hey!" I cough.

"Hey yourself." She smiles. "Your uncle got pulled in all kinds of directions, so I stopped by on my way home. I just want to see how you're doing." She opens the door and greets the therapy team.

After my session, I walk back out into the blistering cold and Dr. P is still waiting for me. She offers to drop me off at home and I jump at the ride because it is freezing outside, and winter isn't forgiving me for wearing a simple pair of jeans without the obligatory leggings or tights underneath. We talk about what it's like growing up in Brooklyn, and Dr. P gives me tips on where to buy leggings that won't break the budget. We're so busy talking that I don't notice Dr. P is already turning onto my block and pulling up to my front door, a steel-gray building sprawled in the middle of the street. It is gated and the branches are bare and shivering.

At the end of the gate is an opening to the trash and recycling bins. Big black steel cages to keep the rats and raccoons at bay. Dr. P uses her emergency signal to double-park as I climb out of the car.

"Let me know if you need anything."

"Thanks, Dr. Patterson. I appreciate the ride home."

"Anytime, Angel," she sings as I close the door and walk up the five steps to the black door. She drives away in the sleek black sedan after a quick honk. It dawns on me that I didn't have to give her directions to Uncle Spence's apartment.

Allow Me to Reintroduce Myself

My arm is still a little tender, but I blame it on my new hobby—I begin making my own playlist. The first two I keep private and refuse to let anyone hear. The most recent one is a mixture of the deep grooves of Erykah Badu and Kehlani, the quick wit of J. Cole and Wale, and the southern slump of DaBaby mixed with the dense rhythm of Burna Boy. I find a conga drum and use it as a segue between songs.

I title my new playlist *Super Feels* and upload it. This is the one I make public. This is when my palms sweat. Both hands a pool of "am I doing this right?"

I have to make a DJ name for my page though. And at first I'm nervous, I don't want it to be wack. It needs to be a mix. A name acknowledging who I used to be, and a welcome to who I am becoming. I am becoming someone that moves when she feels like it. I trust myself, I like my friends, I've found new interests, and I feel like I am in control of my destiny. For once.

I rename myself DJ Angel Reign. My avatar is an image of a red sky with a sun nearly touching the water. When you look at it you can't tell if the sun is rising or falling.

Ting

I was so busy uploading my playlist this morning that I am almost late for school. I walk in late, still listening to the mix, and get all the way to my seat in the circle before I realize Eva is speaking to me. I remove an earbud. "Hey, girl, sorry. What did you say?"

"What you listening to?" Eva inquires before taking my hanging pod and putting it near her ear.

"Just, ah . . . ," I begin, a bit flustered. She bobs her head and closes her eyes for a couple of seconds, which feels like forever before she opens her eyes and smiles.

"This is dope!" She nods along to the beat. "I ain't heard that Kehlani mix before." She hands me back the pod. "Where can I hear it?" She opens her phone and looks up quizzically.

"It's just on my little playlist," I say as I turn off the phone and roll up the earbud cord. I tuck it into my pocket and try to turn her attention away from my playlist and onto our group project.

"Angel." Eva just stares at me. She narrows her eyes and fixes my coat collar like an older sister might. "What's going on, girl? You actin' real jumpy."

I haven't told anyone about my new love for making music playlists. It's like I've learned a new language and every day I'm trying to perfect my vocabulary. I feel like I should keep it a secret just for me right now.

"Girl. It's nothing," I repeat. "I'm good." And my arm starts hurting. A tiny pain stretches from my shoulder blade and plants its roots near my heart.

Last day before break and I need a new book to read. Uncle Spence has to work the early shift of Thanksgiving but promises we'll have dinner with friends the night before. He says to call it Friendsgiving. He says it makes more sense thinking about the Indigenous people who this land belongs to. "We're on unceded land. This land belongs to the Lenape tribe," he once told me when walking around Prospect Park. I figure with my downtime I'll sleep in, make another playlist, maybe walk by the garden if it isn't too cold. Today on my way to school JiggyStax dropped a new playlist called *Eastern Parkway Ting* and I stop in my tracks. *"WTH?"* I whisper out loud to myself. "Come on, yo!" someone insists behind me, and I realize I got to keep it moving or the pileup in the school entrance might get out of hand.

The morning bell is due to ring and the steady flow of students coming into the building, rushing to get out of the cold, couldn't care less about a playlist. I drop my phone and earbuds in the thick pocket of my down jacket, pull off my gloves, and stomp my feet on the carpet by the security desk before showing my ID. I pass Mrs. B's office on the way to class, catch her eye, and wave as I head to homeroom.

The room is empty when I first walk in. I want to ask Ms. G about new book titles. The other day I went to use my library card for the first time, and I met a librarian who threw my whole vibe off. She asked me had I read the classics and when I shook my head she scoffed, "You must read *Moby Dick,* it's a classic!" She handed me a book with a big white whale on the cover. The thin white letters, bold along the top, read: MOBY DICK. I held the book and read the back before shaking my head. I wasn't into the storyline. I used to think it was something wrong with me, not wanting to read certain books that everybody said were the best or were classics. Now I know the truth. "I'm looking for stories that remind me of me. And I don't want to read about anything being hunted or killed."

The librarian flipped her long ash-blond hair and repeated slowly, like I didn't hear her the first time, "But this book is a classic. Reading is all about going to places you've never been."

I kissed my teeth. The same way I learned while waiting in line for beef patties on Franklin Avenue or curry chicken on Fulton Street. The same way I watched a girl rocking skintight jeans and fur-rimmed UGG boots respond to the catcalls when waiting for the uptown 4 train at Utica Avenue.

I pulled my lips back from my teeth and released the sound so loud I surprised myself. She jumped a bit when I began, "Well, my teacher says whatever book that makes you feel like you are home can be a classic." I planted my feet. "My teacher says, 'There are so many homes taken from Black and brown and Indigenous people that sometimes it takes a story to find the voices we thought we lost.'" She lifted her eyebrows but remained silent. Deep inside, something bright broke open in my chest and the tingling-arm sensation ran across my back and shoulders. I handed her back the tattered book with the figure of a whale lurking beneath the water and added, "I'll find another classic."

Ms. G walks into the room, holding a Valentine's Day decorated coffee mug and talking easily to the math teacher, Ms. Ford, as I look at her book collection. Ms. Ford is dressed in a white oversized Toni Morrison sweatshirt and doesn't look like what you might think a teacher is supposed to look like. She rides a motorcycle to school, wears leather boots and red-black-and-green knitted caps over her golden dreadlocks. She has a serious voice, like she owns a business or makes people pay their bills on time, but she always greets students as if they are friends. And she always leaves her classroom door open, even during lunch, if anyone needs assistance on a math problem. She is one of the coolest teachers at Banneker (singing rap lyrics during assembly) and teaches algebra and trigonometry. Eva says Ms. Ford is her favorite teacher and she can't wait to take her calculus class during her senior year. Ms. G waves and puts her coffee mug on the desk before untangling a pair of sun-bright-yellow earrings swinging from her left ear. "Morning, Angel, you ready for another book?" she asks.

I nod before moving my attention back to her collection of new and familiar worlds. My hands brush the neat row of book spines in silence.

In one hand I am holding a copy of Toni Morrison's *Sula* and in my other hand I hold Tayari Jones's *Silver Sparrow.* I open the covers and read the perfectly typed index cards. Each word unfolds a new landscape I've yet to visit but is in my blood, like it's a story for me. I am reading closely to figure out which book I want to borrow when Nikki walks in. Ju Ju is trailing her like a shadow. They both wear the same-colored sweatshirt, but neither of them looks angry.

It's been weeks since the outburst between Nikki, Ju Ju, RaChelle, and Kamilah. Nikki didn't come back to school for the rest of the week. Kamilah said Nikki only posts inspirational quotes about leaving your ex and how to be a "boss bitch who loves God." Ju Ju came to school every day that week, silent as a ghost and her grief hot as fire. She stayed to talk to Ms. G every class and returned each morning with the same air around her, until today.

Reina walks into the classroom, followed shortly by Kamilah, then RaChelle. RaChelle hasn't talked much in class since the incident. She only replies with a random number and a shrug. Ms. G is never rattled. She nods and moves on. Kamilah looks over her shoulder at RaChelle standing in the door and rolls her eyes. Kamilah walks over to greet Ms. Ford, Reina sits in her usual seat in the circle of chairs, and Teiya slides past the doorframe, past RaChelle and her boyfriend, Marshall.

Ever since the fight, RaChelle's boyfriend, Marshall, has walked her to homeroom, arm in arm, like an ad for a sale on junior prom photography packages. Marshall is a short-statured guy with twists and Malcolm X glasses. He chews his gum loud and always looks in the room to make his presence felt. RaChelle finally walks in, but not before hugging him extra-long and making a show out of it. It's like they want everyone to watch, but I've seen this reality TV show before and it gives me chicken skin. I change the channel. I plop open a book or if Eva makes it to school before the bell, I talk to her about anything else.

Eva and I have gotten into the habit of sending each other links of what we were reading or watching online the night before. Eva sends links for documentaries about BLM, DTP, Ferguson Uprising, and some other groups fighting for justice in the communities. In return I send her home videos from some rapper in the Bay Area or a TikTok of a kid dancing with a dog on beat—it keeps us balanced. Eva and I have become real friends. I only ever had Amir as a true friend until I moved here. Now we barely get to text. Maybe a call here and there on the weekends; he's too busy with his new life at school.

I don't talk to Elena. I'm still upset. I just can't figure out if I'm upset with her or myself. She talks to Uncle Spence every other day. Sends me messages of her love through Uncle before I can say I'm too busy to talk. She knows me so well.

Eva has a great relationship with her mom, Nicole Amor. Her mom is a designer and owns a boutique in Bed-Stuy. She repurposes clothing and creates one-of-a-kind wearable art pieces; it's where Eva says she got her swag. I envy Eva's easy relationship with her mother. I envy her ability to talk about ideas that seem too large for me to grasp in one setting. But she never makes me feel dumb. It is the first time in my life that I don't feel ashamed.

About Lasagna & Insta

I sign up for a new IG account so I can watch Eva's IGTV videos explaining the MTA fare increase, or climate change, or her relationship to "womanism in the age of bad feminism and the power of Roxane Gay." I also follow a couple of gossip pages, but that really is to make sure I don't look like a creep. I don't put anything up on my IG page except the same avatar from my SoundCloud page. (I prefer to move in silence, like Lil Wayne's lyrics about lasagna.) Last night I made my sixth playlist; I built up the confidence and sent a link of my page to Eva. I have to keep myself from biting my nails! I'm so anxious to hear what she thinks. I mean, I'm not as good as JiggyStax, but I feel like I got a whole mood. A whole vibe. And what does she say? Nothing. Not a heart emoji. Not the bright red 100 emoji. NOTHING. I fall asleep waiting for her response.

So, when we are finally sitting in front of each other, the day before Thanksgiving break, I can't wait. I'm sitting with Tayari Jones's novel in my lap when Eva walks in wearing sunshine yellow and bright red lipstick. She arrives only minutes before the bell rings. I look at her and suck my teeth. "OMG what do you think?!"

She pretends she doesn't notice me. "Stop playing," I whine.

She smiles, brighter than her outfit, and looks me over. "I love your new braids." She clicks open her phone.

"Thanks," I say, and pat the part of my scalp that's still tingling from the fresh crisscross cornrow braid design. "So," I begin slowly. "What did you think?"

She lifts the face of her phone and shows me that she's following me on her SoundCloud. I grab her phone and squeal as she starts clapping her hands together excitedly. My heart almost bursts. I pass her back her phone and put the book in my backpack to busy myself. I smile like a teeth-whitening commercial.

"I didn't know you were on here like this, sis! Imma tell everybody to follow your page!"

"You don't have to shout me out," I laugh. Look at the screen of her phone and smile even bigger. I have exactly twelve followers, which are probably just bots.

She turns on the camera, selfie style, and starts recording. "Check out my favorite DJ, my homegirl, DJ Angel Reign!" Her voice fades as she faces the camera toward me and then moves next to me back in the frame, hugging my neck. "Don't sleep on my girl, y'all! Stop whatever it is you're doing—watch this video and go follow her now! She's going to hold us down for the youth convention right here in Brooklyn this coming February! Be ready to turn up for justice, y'all! Stay tuned! Peace!" She chucks the deuces, presses stop, adds filters and the BLM emoji. She tags my page and clicks send in seconds.

My mouth falls open. The room starts to spin a little and I lean back in the chair. The room doesn't just start to close in. It crashes.

"Oh no, I can't do this, Eva! I just make playlists for me to figure out how I'm feeling, you know?"

And her face freezes. "Angel, you're an artist. That's why you're always silent and thinking. I get it now," she says quietly. "My mom is an artist. I watch her sometimes when she doesn't realize. She can be cooking and laughing and drinking wine, and the next thing I know she's sitting next to the window and looking out and crying. Look"— she puts her phone in her lap—"if you don't want to, you don't have to. But I would love for you to DJ the afterparty. I listened to the playlists, and they are dope . . ." Her voice trails off and she says in the smallest voice I've ever heard from her, "I mean, I'll delete the video if you want, but promise me you'll think about it, okay? I just want to see you shine."

The room isn't in full spin, but it's a little wavy. I cover my head with the hoodie beneath my jean jacket and count one-to-five, then backward five-to-one. My shoulders loosen and my fingers stretch across the knee patch on my cargo pants. Eva picks the phone up off her lap to delete the post, when I nod and say, "Don't delete the video. I'll think about it."

Teiya sits silent, watching our interaction without an expression on her face. She looks out the window, like she is waiting for the weather to change its mind too.

"This is our last class before break. How's everyone feeling?" Ms. G asks. The bell's cylinder cymbal is still reverberating in the air and Ms. Ford has already left the room. Everyone is silent. Kamilah looks at Reina. Reina looks at Teiya. Teiya looks at RaChelle. RaChelle looks at Eva. Eva looks at me. I look at Ju Ju. Ju Ju looks at Nikki, and Nikki just breathes in slowly. It's as if she is meditating. Or praying. Ms. G looks at Nikki, who is now mumbling under her breath and toying with a golden cross necklace peeking from beneath her sweatshirt.

Nikki breathes out and opens her eyes. "I feel like I'm at an eight. I've been praying for the ability to forgive Ju Ju. She's my best friend. But no lie, she really hurt me. Before being in this group, I never really thought about my feelings. I just reacted to everything and didn't care. I've been going to Mrs. B after school too. She's hooked me up with an internship at her church. They have a fresh LGBTQ teen group and I think I need to just be in a quiet place for a little while."

Ms. G says, "Thank you for sharing, Nikki, and I'm glad you are getting what you need." She gives a slow nod. "Ju Ju?"

"I'm good, Ms. G. I'm about a nine." And for once Ju Ju isn't all "rah rah" with her voice. She plays with the fitted cap sitting on her knee. She isn't loud and boisterous, just a bit still. "I've been thinking about the promises I made to Nikki and to myself. I had all my ideas running around in my head and I've been trying to catch them with all these baskets, but the baskets got holes in them, you know?"

The room nods. "I mean. I got to focus. And I thought if I checked off all the boxes, I mean really stay fixated on what I was getting done, then I would be happy. But I haven't been able to really be happy, because I was looking for my happy in people and things. You feel me?" She leans forward and looks at RaChelle.

"I'm sorry, Ra," she spits out.

Nikki's eyes remain on the ground, while Ju Ju, kind of pleading, looks at RaChelle.

RaChelle is as surprised as the rest of the group and just blinks in disbelief. "We've been over. We were never good for each other, and I shouldn't have put you in that position. I shouldn't have lied to you either, Nikki." Ju Ju turns her attention to Nikki and shakes her head. "I don't know if we'll ever be good. I mean, I want you to trust me. But I understand I'm a lot to deal with." She sits back. "But I'm a good person, Ms. G," Ju Ju adds.

"Yes, you are," Ms. G agrees warmly.

"I just got to do better." Ju Ju breaks into a full grin. "That's what you said, right?"

"Right." She pauses. "And I meant it."

"Word. So, I'm going to do right, nahmeen?" Ju Ju's swagger has returned. "But I'm giving myself permission to still be lit, just with no expectations from anyone else."

Nikki falls into Ju Ju a little and then back into her chair.

"I was a six coming here this morning, because I was nervous and full of anxiety. And then Eva hyped me up and I was a ten. Then she asked me to DJ a party, and I spun out back down to like a six. Which I guess means I'm an average of about an eight?"

"Oh!" Ms. G laughs a little. "Take your time, Angel."

I take a deep breath. "I've been here for almost three months now. This is the first time that I feel like I want to see what happens next. You know? Before, I just went with whatever was thrown at me. I'd been watching my little brother and sisters, I had a toxic relationship with my ex, I didn't really respect my mom, and I haven't talked to my father in years. I move here and I'm just floating around, a damn sling and pain shooting through my shoulder because I don't know how to let go when something or someone isn't good for me."

I lean forward. "It's like, I fell into new things—things I didn't know I could care about—and for the first time it's exciting. You know, I didn't have this back home. Everybody I went to school with, most of them I've known since grade school. And it's still like they didn't know me at all. People had their ideas about me and my mother. And I just fought so much because I was numb. I hate that part of my life. I hate who I became. I was tired of being bullied and gossiped about. But everyone treats girls like me like this. Like we're disposable. You know? That's why I don't care about compliments or gifts. I just want to feel the sun on my face and not worry about the downpour."

This is the first time I've ever spoken this much. And my chest isn't tight, like it normally is. I run my palm against my fresh set of cornrows and look around, a little nervous.

"Angel, thank you for being so vulnerable," Ms. G says. "I'm so glad you felt like you could share today. I'm so thankful to have someone to talk to about books. And so grateful you're in my class."

"I'm happy for you," Eva whispers, and squeezes my hand. "I feel like I'm a ten. 'Cause my bestie is killing it right now. . . ."

But I can't focus on what she is saying. For the first time in such a long time, I can breathe freely.

Classes run into each other like a bubble-gum blur. There is a fire drill and we have to spend an entire period outside in the cold. This is the first time I decide I hate winter. There are flurries coming down and my class is situated next to Nikki's drama class. On the other side of the drama class is a gym class and the only reason I can tell is because they're all wearing their designated dark-gray sweat suits beneath large winter coats. I notice Sterling against the gate with a bunch of guys and begin to walk over. He is already watching me and meets me halfway, a couple feet from some younger boys in his group.

"Hey," I say, feeling brave. During Advisory, I felt a vault door in my body unhinge. I am tired of playing it safe. I am tired of keeping my head down. I want to just be.

"What's up, Angel?" He smiles, walking closer to me. We are an arm's length away and I am warmer already.

There is a group of guys who mimic Sterling's voice. "Heyyyy." Their voices rise an octave.

"Grow up," he responds sternly over his shoulder. "What's going on with you?" he asks, eyeing me curiously. "I haven't really talked to you since . . ." He stalls. "Our walk."

"Yeah, I know. I've been trying to stay busy and keep my focus," I reply honestly. "Moving here and trying to catch up on a whole new life, it's a little overwhelming."

"Word." He nods. He rubs his hands together to fight back the cold. His breath is a mist cloud of warmth and peppermint. "What about now? Are you still overwhelmed?" he asks, looking around as if he isn't bothered by the cold.

"I'm still figuring it out." I laugh, looking directly into his eyes, and fight my nerves to run back to my side of the court. I look up to the sky. Even with the cold biting at my cheeks, I marvel at the snow coming down. It's kind of beautiful. Each snowflake its own mixture compound of hydrogen and oxygen. Each snowflake its own molecular structure. I close my eyes and let a couple of flurries fall into my lashes. "Tell me the truth," I say, my eyes still closed. "Are you DJ JiggyStax?" I open my eyes to search for an answer.

Before Sterling can answer Biz walks up. "What's up, Angel?" The fire drill bell rings, calling us all back into the building for class.

I sit back against the library books and wait for Teiya. She arrives almost immediately. She is carrying two cups of chai in tan-flowered insulated cups with brown lids. She hands me one and sits next to me, cross-legged. I take off the top, blow at the heat, and sip slowly. "Thanks, Teiya, what do I owe you?" I ask.

"You're welcome," she replies, ignoring the question. She pulls a sandwich out of her tote bag, which reads: I LIKE BIG BOOKS AND I CANNOT LIE. I giggle.

"Whatcha eating?"

"Peanut butter and banana sandwich." She takes a bite. "You want one?" I shake my head. My stomach is still flipping since the fire drill.

"It's my favorite," she adds, chewing silently. She pulls out a bag of chips and a small container filled with diced broccoli heads and carrots.

"Are you still reading that big book?" I ask. Sip on the hot, spicy liquid and straighten my cargo pants leg.

"Marlon James?" she asks. "Yep, finished it last night."

My mouth drops open. "But it was like six hundred pages!" I exclaim.

"Six hundred forty!" she corrects me, laughing.

"I don't know how you do it. You just got that book like a week ago! I can't keep up, T. Two hundred pages and it's like I ran track or something! My brain hurts, even when the book is so, so good." I sip the chai, giggling.

"I don't know. I guess I'm just used to reading." She takes another bite of her sandwich.

"Are you excited for the break?" I ask.

She nods. "I get to see Grandy for the first time all year. She is my favorite person but ever since my grandfather passed two years ago, she's moved back to Jamaica to live with her sister n 'em."

During Advisory, Teiya talked about her paternal grandmother visiting from Jamaica. How her father whisked around the house all week preparing his childhood home in East Flatbush until it was "just so." When she talked about her grandy, a different side shined through. She was still quiet, but her eyes danced with excitement. "Oh! And the gud food she makes!" As she counted on her fingers, "rice and peas with coconut milk, sorrel, callaloo, curry chicken, stew chicken, oxtail, curry goat," the group started oohing and aahing and rubbing their bellies.

Kamilah laughed and whispered, "Bring me a plate."

"How about you? What do you have planned?" she asks. And I shrug.

The thing is, I've never been big on holidays. Elena worked so much that me and Amir did our own thing. The triplets were still young, but mostly they were at their dad's house. I envied their other life. Where everything was clean and neat. Our house was a hodge-podge of old and worn items and broken things. It wasn't that we broke everything on purpose. It just kind of happened. Elena didn't really care. As long as she had her cigarettes and a six-pack after work, she was content. I look out the window thinking about which bowl of soup I'd get from the local Caribbean bakery.

"You want to come over?" she asks. Her eyes big, round moons.

"T, you are so nice. But my uncle is coming home early from work. He's already planned a special dinner." I think I'll just stay home with this new book and chill. Maybe work on a new music playlist. I pull my earbuds on and start to listen to the mix from JiggyStax—or is it Sterling?

Teiya nudges my shoulder. "You know. I was thinking about what you said in group today," she says with her usual pensive voice. Like she was thinking of every word very closely. Making sure she said the very correct combination. "I think you DJing is a great thing. I think you will be good at it. You may have been treated differently before you got here. But I like that you have an open mind about things. Sometimes, our hearts and minds are too big for the spaces we orbit, you know? Maybe that's why you find certain spaces difficult for you to connect with. You know they say your energy is blocked if your chakras aren't aligned." My eyes must look like two large exclamation points because I have no idea what a chakra is.

"A chakra?" I say, confused.

"It's like meditating. Right? Like when you think about good things, your spirit is lifted. Chakras are the energy field of your body. And when they are balanced your energy is renewed, and you have a different outlook on even the strangest things. Have you ever meditated before?"

I nod and put down the cup. "I listen to meditation exercises on this new app I downloaded. It's pretty cool."

"Do you trust me to try something different?" she asks, finishing her sandwich and tossing the plastic wrap into a brown paper bag. I nod. "Okay. Cross your legs. And sit as comfortable as you can. We are going to just close our eyes and focus on our breathing for thirty seconds. That's it. You willing to try?"

And even though I listen to my app when I'm by myself, I think, *Why the hell not?* I mean, I am just a girl trying to figure out how to "balance my chakras." What's the worst that could happen?

A.   I close my eyes and try not to think about Sterling. . . .
    1.   Stop that.
B.   I close my eyes and try not to think about Biz. . . .
    1.   Stop that.
C.   I close my eyes and think about my last physical therapy session. I think about Uncle Spence and the way his eyes shined as a smile crept onto his face. I think about Uncle's face when I asked him how he really felt about Dr. Patterson. "Dr. P is a different kind of woman, niece. She's supportive and she's a leader. We dated for a little bit, but I had to get my life together and I understood a woman like her could never wait for a dude like me."
D.   I close my eyes and think about Sterling. . . .
    1.   Stop that.
E.   I close my eyes and

The lunch bell rings.

When I walk out of the building after the final class bell all I can see is: Biz standing by the parked cars lining the residential street.

Before I can open my mouth, Biz waves me over. "Yo, can we talk?" His thumbs are tucked into the hooks of his backpack straps.

He moves forward and I nod. We cross the street as the yellow bus double-parks in the middle of the street.

"Yo, I got something for you?" He puts both hands in the pocket of his lime-green hoodie. He pulls out a piece of paper folded into four neat squares. He places the note in my hand.

"What's that?" I stand next to him and look across the street at the school doors to see if Eva has exited yet.

"Read it and holler at me later. My number is in there." He walks away. And I look as his lime-green sweatshirt stands out until he disappears into a group of students. Behind me, the bright yellow doors of our school flap open and closed as students escape, finally done with the day.

The Note Begins

With a heading I've never read before. It goes:

Dear Angel,

I ain't never been called dear by anybody but the older women at Elena's old church. Then it goes:

I've been thinking . . .

Rewind: Before It Went Bad

Darius called me beautiful, sure. But he also called me out of my name when we were arguing. I didn't mind him being angry, I was used to that. But I wasn't used to someone who called me beautiful also calling me nasty names. The final straw was the basketball game at a competing school. I always visited Darius there, even when we were mad at each other. Which became more frequent than I would like to admit. But what love doesn't have problems? A tall, lanky kid visiting from a school somewhere deep in the Valley asked me my name on the way to the bathroom and I told him, "My name is Angel. My boyfriend is waiting for me on the bleachers." He laughed a little. "My bad," he responded. "But just in case y'all break up, my name is Jace." "Not interested, Jace," I said over my shoulder, and walked away. But Darius only saw me look over my shoulder.

Breakout, Two Time

I walk out of the building after the final class bell and text Eva immediately: *Leave the video up. I have never had anyone cheer for me like you. Thank you for that. Thank you for seeing me.* Eva and I were on two different projects during our period together with Mrs. B. She was sent to help the college center and I had to work on more PTA/Town Hall Meeting materials. Now that I have full use of my hands, I am constantly collating meeting materials for Mrs. B.

I'm down the block when my cell phone vibrates. Eva's text reads: *Turn around.*

There, with a fanny pack slung over her shoulder and her manicured nails waving in the air, Eva smiles.

"I thought you were mad at me," she says, walking up to me. I sling my arm around her shoulders and give her a half hug as we walk toward Myrtle Avenue. She's the first person I've hugged since I moved here. The air feels crisper and cleaner than before.

"I wasn't mad," I reply as we walk, our pace a matching pulse. "I think I'm just nervous."

"About what?" she asks, looking at me with a side-eye. "You got great skin. You are considerate about others, and might I add, you have a fly and environmentally responsible wardrobe." She giggles. "And you got me! I got you, sis." My eyes start leaking. "Are you crying?" she gasps.

"No," I lie. "It's too cold out here."

She nods, looks away, but holds on to my arm as we walk toward the bus stop.

Her: I cry all the time. You know there is nothing wrong with crying, right?

Me: When it was just me and my younger brother and sisters—I never cried. I was too busy. When I was at school and people spread rumors about me, or acted like my mother's job was a joke, I never cried. Well, maybe once or twice, but only in the bathroom stall. I just feel like you are strong all the time.

Her: Nah. I'm a cream puff. Like, I was talking to Miles the other day, and, girl, I just started crying. And I don't know why, it just kind of came over me. One minute we're talking about this documentary on child soldiers in Africa and next thing I know, I'm sobbing—like ugly crying! And he was cool about it. He let me cry.

Me: Damn, that's crazy. I mean, it's sad. But what were you thinking?

Her: I think the child soldiers storyline, just watching these kids having to fight for their life without knowing what the next day or next year for them will look like. And how they move with these machine guns that are as big as their bodies! It's massive to think about. You know? My brother, Bryce, died from gun violence; he was only fifteen when he was at the park hanging out with his friends. Just like that, some kids with guns get into a fight and just start shooting. Bryce tried to run and get to the other side of the gate, but he and two others were hit by stray bullets. The other two kids lived, but he died right there. My moms bursts into tears. But it passes in waves. You know? Because when she's done crying, she gets up, dusts herself off, and gets back to being a boss.

Me: I didn't know you had a brother. I'm so sorry.

Her: I was only three years old when it happened, but I still remember him and I miss sharing our Saturday morning cartoons. We have a memorial every year at the playground, next year in November will be the thirteenth-anniversary memorial against gun violence. And the city tried to police the area, let it get all dirty and tried to close it. But my moms wasn't having it! She put together a community task force. They started cleaning it, planting little bushes nearby, they made it a real playground. Kids got involved and now it's kept up by a planning committee in the neighborhood. That's why she bought her space for the boutique nearby. It's only a block away but she says she wanted to be as close as possible to her muses. You know, you never talk about your mom or dad.

Me: All my life I've been taking care of Elena's house. At a very young age, I was bathing and feeding and walking Amir to school. I had no one to take care of me. My mother was fighting with my dad back and forth. I don't remember him being in the house at all. Like, never. Which just became normal. Because when he was there, they fought. Like, *loud* loud. The neighbors called and the cops came at least every other month. Then he was gone. Just gone. Elena started dating the triplets' father, Smith. And he didn't really like our house or me, I guess. Because it was my house! I took care of everything. Then one day, he was just up and gone. And Elena was sick, so sick with the triplets. So, you know . . . I took care of her. I never talk about Elena, because I think I'm angry at her that I never got to be a kid.

Gratitude on a Thursday

I'm itching to make a new playlist. Eva and I texted until Uncle Spence made it home. She is so cool, she let me have my little meltdown and then helped me get back up. She isn't a therapist, but like a life guru. She is like Mrs. B in a teenager's body. Before Uncle Spence and I started to make dinner (can you say fried chicken wings, collard greens, and mashed potatoes?) she texted me in bold letters, **DO NOT READ THE COMMENT SECTION. PROMISE ME. Okay?** *Dang,* I joked. *Fine.* But in the back of my mind, I thought about it. Like, I know people can be cruel. (I went to school with these people.) But I kind of want to see how many people listened to it. I want to know if I made a vibe. I talk myself out of looking at the music app. My stomach growls. Decision made. Food first.

Later that night, the house is quiet (Uncle must've left for work early) as I walk into the kitchen to make a bowl of cereal. Uncle doesn't believe in name-brand cereal. But also, he doesn't believe in nasty cornflakes. I cut a banana, top the bowl with a crazy amount of almond milk. I put the carton in the fridge and peel back the foil of tonight's dinner and grab a cold chicken wing, for extra protein! In the living room, I reach for the remote when I see a note on top. "Going in early, be back for dinner. I'm making baked mac 'n' cheese, don't eat all the cheese! ☻ And don't stay in the house all day. Get some fresh air." I smile. Uncle Spence is always leaving me messages about getting outside and taking walks in the sun and taking my vitamins. It's trippy because I don't remember him like this when he lived in California, but then we had sun all the time. And I was real young. Honestly, I don't think I've ever had anyone leave me notes about "getting air." I plop on the love seat and click on the television.

Idle minds make trouble. So do Twitter fingers. After breakfast I make the mistake of logging on to SoundCloud and reading the comments. At first, folks were really nice. They left comments like, "I love this song." Or another just had firework emojis. And then, there were some mean comments, like "Who listens to this song anymore?" And "What kind of Cali wackness is this?" I text Eva, *Sorry, I looked.*

You know people are haters for fun, don't worry about it, Eva responds quickly. Then three bubbles fill the screen. *You okay?* she asks.

I text back, *Yep. I'm good. I think you're right. No more comment reading.* I turn off the comment section.

That's right, sis. The playlists are dope. You make music for people to feel good. Anyone that can't see that ain't worth a second glance.

I send three heart emojis and turn my phone over. I click onto the JiggyStax page to see if I can find inspiration. Before the third song of the *Angel Eyes* playlist begins, I text Sterling.

Hey, you free to talk?

Him: Is it hard being without your brother and sisters?
Me: A little bit. I miss them, a lot. The triplets would've been running around the backyard screaming or playing hide-and-seek and messing up the kitchen. This is the first time in I don't know how long that I don't have to worry about anyone else but myself. It's kind of weird.

Him: What's so weird about it?
Me: How quiet my house is.

Him: Yeah, Avion keeps us all on our toes over here. What else you been into since you been here?
Me: I've been reading a lot. I never had much time for it before, but it's given me a lot to think about. I got physical therapy for my arm, which keeps me busy, and I've been listening to a lot of playlists on SoundCloud.

Him: . . .
Me: You know you never outright answered my question at the bell. Are you ever going to tell me the truth? Are you DJ JiggyStax?

Him: How'd you figure it out?
Me: At first, I thought *Angel Eyes* was a coincidence. But then *Eastern Parkway Ting* right after we walked back from the roti spot . . . That was it. The West Coast beats and funk tracks

with the Brooklyn Dodger rhythms. It felt like you were talking directly to me. I liked it.

Him: I'm glad you liked it. Who else do you listen to?
Me: DJ Reborn is pretty fresh. I like her blending sounds between Afrobeats and hip-hop.

Him: Yeah, Reborn is dope. She used to teach after-school classes at Banneker. That's where I got my first taste at being a DJ. After her class, I was hooked.
Me: That's how I feel now. I finish a book and I'm excited to make a playlist, like a soundtrack to the way the book made me feel. Is that weird?

Him: Nah, ain't nothing weird about being a creator. We get inspiration from everywhere. I started with playlists, then I began playing around with Technics 1200s, and now I make mixtapes. I'm saving up for a new set. I planned on going to the military when I graduated next year. But sometimes I dream about becoming a DJ and working at Hot 97.
Me: Why the military?

Him: It'll help with college. And our pops went. He died from cancer when I was graduating seventh grade and Kamilah was in eighth. That's why it's just me, Kamilah, Avion, our mom, and Aunt Patty.
Me: I'm sorry to hear that.

Him: Yeah, it sucked for a while. Kamilah was really a daddy's girl and it hit her differently. So she fell into hanging with a different crowd than normal. I found ROTC and she found Avion's father. She was into fighting and skipping school and went from honor roll to truant court. It was Mrs. B who reached out and got her back to school. We were her students when we were younger and my aunt and Mrs. B are close friends. She never gave up on Kamilah. When Kamilah was ready to get back on track, she was pregnant with Avion. But she's a boss. She homeschooled with Mrs. B until she passed her tests to return to school. And she decided to walk the stage because she wanted Avion to be proud.

Me: Avion is such a sweet baby. You can tell he loves you. It makes me miss the triplets. They really drove me crazy, but I can't imagine a world without them. Sometimes I find myself texting my little brother to see if he did XYZ and I remember, I'm on the other side of the country! That's wild, right?

Him: Makes sense to me. My days changed drastically when Avion was born. I remember when we brought him home. It was like there was laughter in our house again. Like somebody opened the curtains and let all the light in.

Rewind: Before

Darius called me beautiful, sure. But he also called me out of my name when we were arguing. I didn't mind him being angry, I was used to that. But I wasn't used to someone who called me beautiful also calling me nasty names. The final straw was the basketball game at a competing school. I always visited Darius there, even when we were mad at each other. Which became more frequent than I would like to admit. But what love doesn't have problems? A tall, lanky kid visiting from a school somewhere deep in the Valley asked me my name on the way to the bathroom and I told him, "My name is Angel. My boyfriend is waiting for me on the bleachers."

He laughed a little. "My bad," he responded. "But just in case y'all break up, my name is Jace."

"Not interested, Jace," I said over my shoulder, and walked away. But Darius only saw me look over my shoulder.

When I walked out of the bathroom after reapplying my lipstick, Darius was fighting Jace near the entrance. Jace was slimmer than Darius, but he wasn't afraid, and they flung each other around the school gymnasium, using the wall to break their fall. The security guard and referees tried to break the fight up. I screamed Darius's name until my voice was hoarse. When they finally were separated, I ran to Darius's side and tried to walk him out. The school patrol was on their walkie-talkies warning the officers in the parking lot of the boys they were kicking out. The mob from both schools surrounded us and we tried to move quick to the car.

Darius snatched his hand away from mine. Called me names and blamed me for this mess. I blamed him for jumping to conclusions and waited near the passenger window for him to unlock the door.

He yelled at me again, "I'm tired of your shit. You really is worth-less!"

He sounds like my father did when he yelled at my mother. I tried to open the door, but it was locked, only the window was partially rolled down. I reached in to unhook the lock and Darius yelled at me again. Told me to find another way home. He pushed the metal pedal and the car sped backward, almost running over the brand-new kicks he bought me. I tried to wrench my hand out the window, but it was too late. My arm was stuck and he pulled me along. Maybe it was a couple of feet. But it felt like eternity. Those few seconds of silence before I screamed in agony. It felt like forever ago, when he held my hand and kept me safe. When he called me *beautiful.* When he treated me like it was him and I against the world. It was so long ago, and the pain in my arm, still jammed in the window, brought me back to this mess of a relationship.

A Letter from Home

Dear Angel,

My beautiful firstborn. I am sorry I relied on you so much. The world sometimes is larger than we imagine, and the next thing you know you have five mouths to feed and a failing relationship. I am working on myself these days. In therapy and church every Sunday. I picked up some extra shifts at the stadium downtown. It's messy work but it keeps me busy. Your sisters are living with their father at the moment and Amir is staying on campus. He comes home once a month and I think that's best until I can become stable again. In church with Sister Nancy, I listen to Bible stories on my phone when I am cleaning. It doesn't bother the school administration, and that's okay with me. I just need something to guide me as I work, you know? I miss you very much. And after talking with the sheriff, I realized how much I relied on you to keep everything in order. You did such a good job, Angel. I am so lucky to have you as a daughter. The way you looked after your sisters, Ayanna, Ashanti, and Asha. The way you have always looked after your brother, Amir. You were so good at holding it all together that I forgot you were a kid too. You were still growing up too. The situation with you and Darius scared me, Angel. It reminded me so much of your father and me. We loved each other, sure. But we weren't good together. And I think the abuse made you believe it was normal. I am sorry for that. I should've done more to protect you. I am trying to be better every day. The triplets and I have a weekly picnic and we are going to have a nice holiday break together. Three days of just the girls; we miss you so much. But I know you are taken care of. Your uncle gives me reports of your activities often. He says he thinks you've found your way nicely there. Do you think about coming home to finish high school next year? Or do you think you would rather stay in Brooklyn? Whatever you decide, I want you to do what you want to do. I'm sure we'll get some coins together to get a plane ticket there and see you—maybe next summer? I'd love to see what your world is like. You know, I've never been to New York City. Are the lights as bright as they say? Is it snowing still? How are you keeping warm? I've sent a gift card with this letter so that you can buy whatever you like for Christmas. And your sisters made a Popsicle-stick picture frame for you! Full of glitter and their beautiful faces. They are strong-minded, like you. And they want everyone to be happy, like Amir. All of you are my greatest accomplishments. I get things wrong a lot, Angel. But with you five, I got it right. I love you. Merry Christmas, baby. I hope to hear your voice soon.

Love always,
Your mother

During the break, I talk to Sterling from night until the sun creeps into the room. I tell him about my past. He just listens and lets me talk. It feels warm, our conversations. I like him but I'm not ready, I tell him bluntly. "It's okay, Angel. This is enough," he offers quietly. And we talk until the sun creeps in my window.

During the break, Uncle Spence invites Dr. P over for Kwanzaa dinner. They hold hands when she arrives, and my stomach flips in excitement. She hugs me gently. Asks me about my arm. I smile and introduce her to Eva, who has already arrived. Uncle begins to bring the main dishes to the table. I set the table for four. Red, black, and green linen, red-rimmed colored glasses for the homemade sorrel (a gift from Dr. P) next to the set of silver utensils framing the red ceramic plates and black bowls for the gumbo. Eva asks if she can plug into the Bluetooth speakers and I nod. She plays my playlist and we laugh and dance in the living room as Uncle and Dr. P bob their heads to the beat. "This you, niece?" Uncle's face lights up like the Rockefeller tree. I nod shy-like.

"This is dope," Dr. P says as they begin two-stepping together. Her thigh-high, suede boots and his suede loafers in step with one another, on beat, together, ride the rhythm.

During the break, I see Biz on the stoops of the Brooklyn Library. We haven't talked much since he wrote me the note. In the note, he wrote, "Dear Angel, I've been thinking about the things I said in the hallway. I ain't mean no disrespect. My bad." Biz is talking to a girl with a short bob and patent-leather Jordans. They are seated on the cold granite but don't look bothered by the brisk air. The girl turns to face me and I realize it's Teiya with a new haircut.

"I love your hair!" I shout from the opposite side of the almost-quiet street.

"Angel, thank you!" And I think she blushes.

"How's your grandma?" I ask.

"She's good. She don't suffer no fools gladly, but neither do I." Biz's eyebrows lift and they both giggle.

"Ight, y'all." I wave and continue walking to the bodega for my Flamin' Hot Cheetos. "See you next semester!" Biz puts a fist in the air, in solidarity, then tosses his arm across Teiya's shoulders.

During the break, I reread my mother's letter like I'm searching for new clues on how to heal a broken heart. I text Amir and he texts back two simple but incredibly difficult words: *Call her.* I give in. I dial her number and she picks up the phone on the second ring. "I've been waiting to hear your voice, Angel."

"Hi, Mom. I love you too. Thank you for the card." And we talk, about yesterday and tomorrow. She talks. I listen. I learn who my mother was and who she is trying to become until the sun sinks low behind the glass dome of the Brooklyn Museum.

During the break, I am invited to celebrate New Year's Eve with Eva and her mom. The whole community gathers to meet at the park for a live DJ'd block party. There are card tables lining the grass with so many snack options: pastelitos, beef patties, vegetarian egg rolls, and small multicolored jugs of fruit punch. Everyone is given a balloon, to memorialize those lost to gun violence, to release into the sky at midnight. Before midnight can strike electric, the music calls us into the center of the green. Some dance with small children saddled on their hips, while others bob their heads and tap their feet in the chairs, sleeping children cradled safely in their laps. When a hundred white balloons rescue the blue-black sky, air horns sound, and joy captures the air before the names of the lost rise above the music. Neighbors kiss both cheeks with well wishes and prayers before the sparklers ignite and shake the park into another round of line dancing. Sterling sends a *Happy New Year!* Mom and Amir send heart and firework emojis to our group chat. Uncle texts, *Happy New Year niece, see you home in an hour?* I answer the text before Eva pulls me into the crowd to do the Cupid Shuffle. My eyes flicker happiness at this new season of joy. My cheeks hurt from all the laughter. I close my eyes and ride the wave, both arms in the air like I'm finally free.

During the break, after the New Year's Eve party, I release my newest playlist inspired by Sterling and our late-late talks. I call it *Brooklyn Beginnings.* I want it to feel the way I feel. Like it is full of possibilities. Like it is full of croon and sweetness. Like the mood I create for my vision board today is for the tomorrow to come. But today is so beautiful, I want it to move people to feel as lit and happy and hopeful as possible. It features all the R&B sounds I feel beneath my sternum. I couple songs from Sade and Luther and Method Man and MF Doom. I got songs from Mary J. Blige to Heavy D, from Alicia Keys to Zo!, from Michel'le and J. Cole; the melodies run into each other like ideas, with nowhere to go but up.

Acknowledgments

Thank you to the counselors, educators, facilitators, librarians, and teachers who go the extra mile. Thank you for your patience and care. Thank you for giving so much to young people despite the system that disregards them under the auspices of budgetary issues. Thank you for every day of the week that you make it to the front of the class, and every single day of the week that you sacrifice for the light dimming behind the eyes of our forgotten youth. Thank you, Brooklyn, the Bronx, Harlem, Queens, Manhattan, and Staten Island, for your public schools. Thank you, public schools. Where would we be without you? You are not championed enough for your resilience, and we owe you more.

This book was not what I thought I would sit down to write—but it has all the touch points of our humanity. I had the space to stretch these stories into being at AIR Serenbe, Baldwin for the Arts, Urban Word NYC, and the island of Antigua. I am thankful for the guidance of Eve Ewing and Amanda Torres.

I am thankful to my editor, Phoebe Yeh. I am thankful to the PRH team: Elizabeth Stranahan and Kristopher Kam. I am grateful to the YA community that checked in on me and always found time to remind me we are not islands. So thank you endlessly and always to:

Jive Poetic, Cristin O'Keefe Aptowicz, Sarah Kay, Jaqueline Woodson, Ayana Walker, Nicole Sealey, Renée Watson, Christina Olivares, Jason Reynolds, Whitney Greenaway, and Tiffany Walters.

I wish us all this kind of love. A family of friends who treat you warmly.

About the Author

Mahogany L. Browne is the executive director of JustMedia, a media-literacy initiative designed to support the groundwork of criminal justice leaders and community members. This position is informed by her career as a writer, organizer, and educator. Mahogany has received fellowships from Agnes Gund, AIR Serenbe, Cave Canem, Poets House, Mellon Research, and Rauschenberg, and she founded the diverse literary campaign the Woke Baby Book Fair. She is the author of *Chlorine Sky,* which received a starred review from *The Bulletin,* calling Mahogany "a remarkable, compelling voice." She has also written *Woke: A Young Poet's Call to Justice, Woke Baby, Black Girl Magic,* the poetry collection *I Remember Death by Its Proximity to What I Love,* and *Vinyl Moon,* a story about how we rebuild ourselves after a terrifying moment and the people we become if we allow ourselves the chance. Mahogany is based in Brooklyn, New York, and is the first-ever poet in residence at Lincoln Center. You can learn more about Mahogany at mobrowne.com.